UNNATURAL ACTS

& OTHER STORIES

Acknowledgments:

"Best in the Business" & "Knockouts" originally appeared in *Close to the Bone,* Silver Salamander Press, 1993. "Flamethrower," Roadkill Press, 1991. "Rush" originally appeared in *Unnatural Acts*, Tal Publications, 1992.

First Richard Kasak Book Edition 1994

First printing February 1994

ISBN 1-56333-181-0

Cover Art by Judy Simonian
Cover Design by Steve Powell

Manufactured in the United States of America
Published by Masquerade Books, Inc.
801 Second Avenue
New York, N.Y. 10017

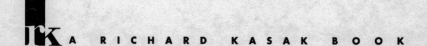

UNNATURAL ACTS

& OTHER STORIES

LUCY TAYLOR

*For Ed, who has inspired more of my erotic
fantasies than are contained within this book*

Unnatural Acts & Other Stories

Introduction

IT'S ALWAYS BEEN my view that the best fiction is that which surmounts trends, market slots, simple escapism, etc., and delves without reservation into new and distressing—and often forbidden—terrains. As a mass-market horror novelist, I collide with such stumbling blocks all the time; I haven't sold my soul yet, but you never know. Instead, I find myself reveling in the creative domains of other, more brazen authors. Indeed, from Joyce to Lawrence to Burroughs, and from Sallee to Acker to Joanou, modern literary history is fecund with fiction whose importance impacts the reader via its sheer aesthetic bravado.

The same thesis struck me, quite squarely, when I began reading Lucy Taylor. I was, and continue to be, floored by the uniqueness of vision I found in this woman's work. It always seems possessed of something more than the mere capacity to entertain, but a very focused and finely tuned capacity to equally provoke, to incite, to make me contemplate far beyond that of typical fiction. In short, Taylor is a writer unlike any other I can name, totally incomparable, totally distinctive, and exclusively terrifying.

And that's what her work is "about" over all: terror. Sheer, unadulterated, triple-distilled *terror*. Taylor rarely pens a super-natural tale; instead, her conception of horror lies rooted in the bedrock of reality, and, more specifically, we're talking *sexual* realities—aspects of concepts, ponderings, and fantasies that all too frequently we refuse to acknowledge to anyone but ourselves. Hence, also, a bedrock of human truth. Here you'll find no haunted mansions (my next novel, by the way, is about a haunted mansion), no lycanthropies or Count Dracula look-alikes, and no aspiring splatter-flick reanimated cadavers. In Taylor's work, the thing that goes bump in the night is more often than not something much more familiar. Our roommates or college chums. The woman next door. That normal-look-ing man we see walking lackadaisically along the beach every day. The last person we fell in love with.

And sometimes, perhaps, even the face that stares back at us in the mirror each morning.

Yes, quite ravenously, and in a disturbingly real, wide-open style, Lucy Taylor introduces us to the new Dark Age, the age of sex and death, of blood and semen, of serial killers and sociopaths, where the real horrors await in the psyches of the very real people around us. In our homes, in our streets, and, par-ticularly, in our beds. And these same horrors quickly outpace the "mainstream," detailing with the precision of an autopsy the most harrowing sexual aberrations; Taylor seems to smash taboos as complacently as punks smash beer bottles on the sidewalk.

Here you'll find a world stripped bare of its specious and feeble veneers—a nightmare world of sexual frenzy and sexual addiction, of obsessive/compulsive love-dementias, of human dreams crushed by human truths, where the flash of a knife or the report of a pistol arrive with the same spontaneity as a kiss. This is hard stuff, yes, and quite ghostly in its own way. But these are the *new* ghosts for the *new* age of fiction. Ghosts such as substance abuse, erotopathy and sadomasochism, autosexu-al asphyxia, child molestation....

And that's just to name a few.

In other words, if you've never read Lucy Taylor, you're in for one rough ride.

Unnatural Acts and Other Stories provides a powerhouse collection, a virtual *compendium* of its namesake. And I'm enthused to proclaim that, in her already extensive list of published erotic horror stories, the ones you are about to read represent Taylor's best and most challenging work to date, and indisputable proof that she's not just a very good writer but, with the '90s as her proving grounds, a devastating one.

—Edward Lee

The Best in the Business

When Arturo first awakened after the avalanche, he was in his bed back in Baton Rouge and his mother was bending over him. She smelled of Tabu and potent Mexican weed. To Arturo, her pale skin and crimson lips made an alarming contrast, reminding him of beads of blood like snow-encrusted rosebuds.

Snow. Vast canopies of it unfurling down the hillside, like someone shaking out a deadly carpet, his companions yelling at him to move and Arturo skiing, skiing for his life, except he wasn't really experienced at back-country skiing—he was only in Winter Park, Colorado, because he had a job to do—and the avalanche kept gaining on him like a tsunami of snow and then that incredible roar, like standing on the runway next to a jumbo jet taking off, and then—night.

Night in the middle of the day.

He had never realized snow could be so black.

But his mother was here. His mother with her racehorse legs and lilting laugh and her way of stroking his cheek ("My sweet, sweet boy") as they sat on her bed, watching the afternoon soaps, which she punctuated with tidbits of motherly advice ("You see that woman, that Melissa, she's the kind of woman to watch out for when you grow up"), and sometimes she'd let him have a sip of her tequila or a toke off her joint.

She never punished him, not even when he lied or stole, because he was all she had now that his father had run off, the only good thing she had done in her life, she used to say.

And when he got older and was too big to punish even if she'd wanted to, he discovered that what people didn't want to give you in this world, you could take if you were just bigger and stronger and willing to hurt them badly enough to get it.

Oh no, Mama, you don't have to worry about women like Melissa. Or anybody else. The world had better worry about me.

Mama, I'm hurt.

She placed her red lips wetly on his forehead, the exact spot where you'd want to put the bullet if you were taking someone out. Her kiss made his skin tingle.

Then he remembered he was forty-eight years old and that his mother had been dead for nineteen years, and fear hopped around in his gut like an infestation of toads.

The fear quadrupled, the toads in his belly leapfrogging level with his heart, when he saw the angel. At least he thought that's what the creature was. Maudie Elway hadn't been much on religious training, but Arturo had gone to Sunday School a time or two before deciding it was for girls and sissy-boys, and Maudie had never forced him to go back.

This angel, though, was definitely not from any Bible School story, more a cross between a celestial divinity on a cathedral ceiling and a silicone-enhanced sexpot from a Fellini wet dream. In place of arms, she had a raptor's silvery wings folded across her upper body like a stripper's plumes, plumping up sufficient cleavage to display the enormity of her bosom. Her white-blonde hair—dazzling hair, sun on ice—fell in deep drifts to her naked shoulders and her pink skin captured the luminosity of palest mother-of-pearl.

The wings fell provocatively short of covering her pubis. Arturo could see the blonde fur of her pubic mound, a radiant down, and the heavy gold rings that pierced the elongated lips of her vulva.

"What is this?" he demanded. "What are you?"

The winged creature offered him a smile as bright and hard as a Times Square whore's and colder than the snow that had thundered down the chute at Berthoud Pass, burying him.

"Hello, Arturo. I'm your Fuckangel."

Arturo sputtered with confusion and disbelief. "My *what*?"

"A Fuckangel," said the being. "An idealized sexual partner, the ultimate fuck, as it were. Everybody has one pictured somewhere in their minds, that face and body that could make you hard or wet for eternity. Even the Pope has a Fuckangel, even Mother Teresa. Not even a saint can say no to a Fuckangel. But unless you're very unlucky, we only appear after death."

"Jesus," said Arturo. "The avalanche. I died in a fucking avalanche. I don't even like to ski. I was just there to do a hit on some ski bum who was balling the wrong guy's gash."

He looked toward his mother for comfort—the angel, whatever it was, was too glaring, too high-voltage sexy, she made Arturo's groin and head throb simultaneously—but his mother's eyes looked waxen, bruised, the work of a taxidermist having a bad day. Arturo had seen that look sometimes on people just before he took them out—numb, defeated, beyond terror.

Whatever it was that could put that look in his mother's eyes, he didn't want to meet it.

"Mama, what is it? Talk to me."

She looked at him with such dread that he tried to sit up and shake her, demand an explanation, but found himself immobile, pressed back down by a terrible weight and a cold that probed along his spine like a blunt scalpel.

"Good-bye for now, Arturo," said the Fuckangel. "But don't worry. You'll see me again." She lowered her radiant head and deep-kissed Arturo's mother. A tremor shivered through the Fuckangel's body. Her wings cocooned tightly around her.

When she unfurled them, the Fuckangel had transformed into an entirely different being.

"Ready, Maudie?" the new creature whispered. Its voice was male now, deep and resonant. Arturo's mother gave a tiny whimper.

The Fuckangel lifted up its wings, revealing genitals of spectacular virility, a massive phallus knobbed like a stalagmite, that bobbed against the lightly feathered belly. The gold rings that earlier had pierced its labia now clanked gently at the penetrated scrotum.

As it embraced Arturo's mother, she seemed to swoon. For a moment, all Arturo could see was her black hair, tumbling into disarray under the kiss of the virile angel. The muscular flanks bucked lewdly. Arturo's mother groaned and broke into piteous weeping. It sounded to Arturo as if she was pleading—for her life perhaps?—he had heard such shameless pleas before. Usually they came from some underworld hireling in disfavor with the mob or a drug dealer turned FBI informant and would begin about the time Arturo made the victim get on his knees, hands behind his neck. He always gave them time to pray. Funny thing was, they rarely prayed to any God. They prayed to him—to Arturo—their executioner. Their prayers were promises and pleas and desperate begging that he might spare their lives.

He never did. That was why he was the best in the business.

But now those same words coming from his mother's throat, *please* and *stop* and *no,* made his stomach convulse and the tone of her voice changed subtly although the words remained the same, so that now *no* began to sound like *yes* and *stop* like *go on forever.*

Afterward, the light was gone from his mother's eyes and her breath came in little ragged gasps, like something hard and jagged was struggling to pass down her birth canal, rending her as it progressed.

"Time to begin," said the angel. Its face had changed, too, the features masculine, but still coldly, glaringly beautiful, the eyes still tourmaline, but avid as a satyr, the jaw straight as the blade of an axe.

The angel gestured with a wing toward the wall opposite the bed where Arturo lay pinned down by excruciating cold. In his real room in the home of his boyhood, that wall had been papered with pictures of dinosaurs and astronauts and even, as he got older, the centerfolds his mother pretended not to see. Now it was bare and viscous gray, like the puke of an anorexic. As Arturo watched, images moved and changed upon it like the shifting shapes of clouds.

His mother and the Fuckangel watched, too. As soon as Arturo realized what they were viewing, he swore and tried to distract his mother. Jesus, she mustn't see the things he'd done! She'd loved him blindly, after all, oblivious to his appetite for cruelty. It was she who had convinced him he was special, entitled to whatever he wanted in the world, whether he'd earned it or not.

Now she tried to turn away, but the Fuckangel tilted her chin up, began caressing the length of her body. As the angel's touches grew more intimate, strange sounds emerged from Maudie's mouth, sounds Arturo found almost as sickening to hear as the scenes on the wall must be terrible for his mother to view.

Arturo was forcing a man and a woman into the trunk of a car. The woman struggled and he had to whack her across the jaw with the side of his gun to get her to go in, while the man begged and tried to make a deal. The car was white, a late model Eldorado, the landscape that of the desert outside Tucson, the banshee silhouettes of the saguaros rising up like exclamation points to punctuate the bleakness.

Arturo remembered hiding his rental car half a mile away and walking to where the two sat in their car, killing a six-pack while they waited for an Arthur Morrisett of Miami to arrive to buy four kilos of cocaine. The man was Mexican, little more than a mule, but an ambitious mule who'd skimmed too much of his boss's profits, the woman his unfortunate companion.

The woman was sobbing now, and so was Arturo's mother, but the images kept unfolding, relentless and horrific: Arturo siphoning gas out of the Eldorado's tank, ringing the car with it before he tossed the match. The Eldorado going up like raw meat on a spit and the sounds from within the trunk—had he really been able to hear the screams so clearly the first time?—as the two fried alive inside their metal coffin.

"Arturo? Arturo, sweetie? Is that an erection I see?"

He squirmed with shame, like the time his mother'd caught him beating his meat into one of her bras. At least jerking off was normal for teen-aged boys. But did she guess he always got a hard-on when he killed someone, that when he torched the Eldorado his dick had been stiff as a crowbar, hot as a hound on the trail of blood? Did she guess it was the sexual rush he got from inflicting pain that *really* made him the best in the business?

"Sweetheart, I'm so very sorry," she was saying, her heart-shaped face pressed near his, the pungency of the pot smell overpowering her perfume. "I have to do this. He says I must."

Before Arturo fully realized what she was doing, he felt the surge of heat. Flames bloomed like roses in his mother's hands—she was juggling fire—as, with a cry, she tossed her gaudy bundle onto Arturo's bed. In an instant, it became a roaring funeral pyre, flames gnawing up his shins, skinning the flesh from his penis and groin, fire suckling at his neck like flame beasts nursing. He howled as the fire found his mouth, rammed its way inside and poured down his throat while tongue and gums and tonsils crisped like deli meats. His eyeballs bulged, then toasted as the flames consumed him down to charred bone and blackened mementos of flesh and still he lived and still he heard his mother weeping.

He lived. This, above all, appalled him. Anyone who charted such new territories of suffering surely had a right to die.

Yet within moments, it seemed, his gruesome injuries had healed, and the wall writhed again with its obscene images. His mother now looked smaller, older, her eyes deeply sunken wounds. The Fuckangel kept a wing protectively around her, caressing its silky-looking feathers across her face.

Now Arturo recognized Buddy Mendoza, who had fucked over a very important Italian gentleman to the tune of about three hundred thou in '89. "Have fun with the scumbag," his employer had said, and did Arturo know how to have fun! He got out the Handy Home Repairman's Tool Kit that an old girlfriend had once given him on the mistaken assumption that he was good at fixing things. Well, not really. He was good at taking things apart. Which was what he did to this Mendoza creep, piece by piece, with wrenches and pliers and drill.

He had wondered at the time if he should write the Handy Home Repairman's Tool Kit company a letter of endorsement for their excellent product, including the truly astonishing potential of their Phillips screwdriver as a proctoscope.

The torturing of Mendoza, Arturo discovered, was a lot less fun the second time around and seemed to last much longer.

Through it all, the Fuckangel was fondling Maudie, murmuring in her ear, stroking aside the hair to kiss the damp back of her neck, wedding the erotic and the tender with the unspeakable and ghastly. Arturo could see her shoulders quaver, hear her hiccoughy sobs above the obscene gurgling noises Mendoza made.

But when the scene was finally finished and the woman who had claimed to love him more than life itself stepped toward him, Arturo could only utter the kind of desperate, babbling pleas he'd heard from many of his victims.

"Please, Mama, don't. Don't do this. You don't want to do it. I know you don't."

"I must," she said. "He wants me to."

"No, you don't. You love me. I'm your son."

"I have to," she said. "I have to please him or he won't fuck me anymore," and this time he despised her for how weak she was, how pitiful, always needing a man, although he had thought he was the man she needed. "I'm sorry," she said as the wrench's strong jaws seized him like a pitbull made of metal, and blood spewed as Maudie Elway began to dismantle her son.

When it was over, there was a brief respite, in which Arturo plummeted through a cold, white pain so complete and terrible that the sheer excess of suffering left him numb. Then the Fuckangel kissed his mouth and changed into its female form, all honey and musk and curves, and licked his mutilated body, tongued his stumps and gouges. Her touch brought his body back to life, but it wasn't that she sought to pleasure him but to sensitize him once again to pain. No sooner did her caresses stir him than the agony returned, and she left him to his suffering.

During those times when the female Fuckangel wasn't with him, Arturo could watch the male version of the creature with his mother, a winged beast of indomitable virility, rending Maudie from behind, and the Fuckangel would grin at Arturo over his mother's raised rump as if to say, "She's mine now, buddy. You'll never get her back. I've fucked her wits out, and she'll never be your Mom again."

When the pictures began to show up on the wall again, the angel buried his gorgeous head between Maudie's thighs and, though Arturo couldn't see her face, he knew she watched, and she wasn't crying now at all, but shuddering with high-pitched laughter that sounded like the glee of the insane.

This time the scene showed a much younger Arturo, just out of high school, and there was that snotty math teacher Miss Arguellez, who'd called him an ignorant punk and failed him twice in Algebra. He'd caught her staying late to grade papers, and he didn't just rape her—that would have been too easy, too good for her—but hauled her into the coat closet by the hair and drummed his fists into her belly until she bled inside and gouts of blood spat up out of her throat while Arturo sent her into the next world impaled on the dick of her killer.

"No, please," whimpered Miss Arguellez.

"No, please," said Arturo's mother, and the Fuckangel whispered in her ear and put something in her hands.

"Yes, I guess it would be fun," Arturo heard her say, "but why not let me do it to someone else? My father or my brother. Anyone except my son."

But the Fuckangel frowned like an angry Zeus and fluttered its great wings as though getting ready to fly away. Arturo knew his mother wouldn't be able to resist, she'd never be able to let go of such a stud, angel or not. Still he tried, he pleaded with her for mercy, but she was already at work, looping the wire around his testicles as though she'd been in the business of torture all her life.

And, definitely, she had an aptitude, for when she pulled the wire taut just as the Angel entered her, his mother smiled.

Blood-red, howling, star-spangled agony sent the pain centers of Arturo's brain into exploding overload. He bucked against the smothering weight that pinned him, bit through his lower lip so that blood squirted from between his teeth, but that pain was paltry, nothing. *Please stop.* Then Arturo's mother lifted up that part of him that was still intact, and went to work again while the Fuckangel thrust on. That tiny part of Arturo's mind still capable of registering something beyond pain and fear understood then that the Fuckangel was no angel at all, but a gorgeous demon who'd corrupted his mother down to the roots of her soul.

When it ended—Arturo babbling gibberish and biting a bloody trench in the back of his wrist—his mother was huddled weeping on the floor, arms locked around her knees, face hidden beneath the fall of hair that had gone ash-white, her front teeth chewing her lower lip into a raspberry pulp. The Fuckangel kissed Arturo quickly on the forehead and sexchanged so fast he could almost imagine the flood of estrogen rushing through her angel's blood as her penis downscaled into a clitoris, her heroic pectorals swelled to D-cup breasts.

Her smile, scaldingly bright, blazed down on him. Arturo cringed and wriggled as though skewered on her stare.

"Keep away from me," he babbled. "I know what this is. I never believed in it before, thought it was just a bunch of stories meant to scare people, but I know now. This is Hell, and you're some kind of devil sent to torture me. That's it, ain't it?"

The Fuckangel laughed, a melodic trill that degenerated into a rasp. Her lovely face changed once again, became a slack-faced, leering demon. Ringlets of decomposing flesh dripped from her skull, the top of which was coming into view like an island exposed by low tide. She bent and forced a kiss like coals upon Arturo's mouth. Her breath smelled of excrement, her eyes were sightless as a corpse with pennies in its eyes.

"Wrong, Arturo," the transformed angel croaked. "As usual, you think the world revolves around you, that even Hell revolves around you. That's not the case. This isn't your hell…it's your mother's."

She smiled her reeking smile. Her coin eyes glittered.

Suddenly Arturo was plunging down the snow chute, the din of the avalanche battering his ears, the great wall of snow looming behind him, and he knew that he could no more out-run it now than he had the first time. The avalanche swept up and over him, making kindling of his legs and pulverizing his ribs, snuffing out his sight, but in the icy dark under eight feet of snow, he could still see the Fuckangel. She was in the process of transforming again. Instead of feathers, her white wings were made of icicles. Her hair was black, her full lips scarlet, her breath the familiar-as-apple-pie perfume of tequila and primo weed. "Your hell starts now, Arturo," the Maudie-Fuckangel crooned. "And remember, I'm the best in the business."

Baubo's Kiss

It was being angry at C.J. more than any spirit of adventure that drove Mira to go off alone to explore the island that day in early summer. Not that there was much to see on Kirinos. The small Ionian island was the sixth in a string of islands that she and C.J. had visited, some more flat or mountainous or lushly wildflowered than others, all redolent with heat and goat piss and retsina. So far, Kirinos was the least promising of the lot. Something about the people, Mira decided, as she pedaled the rented Schwinn along the dirt track that led away from the town. They seemed a glum and lifeless lot, not just more taciturn than the townsfolk she and C.J. had encountered on the other islands, but downright moribund.

The heat, perhaps, thought Mira, as sweat scrawled long itchy lines along the cracks between her breasts and buttocks. You could fry squid on the rocks here (and judging from some meals she'd had, maybe that was what they did), and it was barely ten o'clock.

Yet she pedaled on, determined to find something of interest or note to justify such an expenditure of energy on so blistering a day.

C.J.'s energy, as usual, was being vigorously conserved, unless you counted the hoisting of glass to lips to be a form of weight training. If so, Mira figured her lover would have set some sort of record for elbow-bending by the end of their vacation.

She'd left C.J. slouched at one of the ubiquitous waterfront tavernas, nursing a hangover with what, to Mira, seemed an unlikely remedy—a glass of ouzo and a plate of stuffed grape leaves and *taramosalata,* a gummy-looking paste of smoked fish roe.

But then, despite what Mira thought was an unseemly love of drink and indolence, C.J. seemed to require no exercise to maintain a body that was both athletically lean and pleasingly curvaceous.

Whereas I, thought Mira with not a little envy, *could pedal from here back home to Scranton and still have a bum like a wench in a Bruegel painting.*

Not for the first time, Mira wondered what C.J. saw in her—a fat and dowdy bookworm with plain, freckled features and eyes that squinted myopically from behind heavy lenses. Perhaps it was that C.J. felt her own good looks were shown to best advantage next to Mira's plainness, that her own extroversion sparkled with more brilliance contrasted with Mira's shyness. The idea of being a mere foil to highlight her lover's sex appeal made Mira pedal harder, fueled by despair and self-disgust.

At least, she thought, by way of preserving some modicum of self-esteem, *I'm out and about, exploring something besides the beer and wine list.*

Trying to, at any rate.

The reality was, so far at least, Kirinos seemed as stolid and uninviting as its citizenry. On both sides of the dirt track, olive groves stretched to a flat, unpromising horizon. Bands of scrawny, brown and white goats eyed Mira from the shade of stunted trees, but her passing was acknowledged only by a ribby dog, who came lunging at her rear tire with unnerving, if short-lived menace, before sensibly retreating to the shade.

Still, as her surroundings gave Mira more and more reason to feel discouraged, she pedaled resolutely on. She'd spent much of the last nine months cooped up in the Bodleian Library at Oxford, studying for an M.A. in Greek and Roman literature. Her pasty skin and pudgy thighs attested to her scholar's dedication. Now she had three weeks of freedom before summer classes started. Hot and weary though she might be, she wasn't going to be like C.J. She was damn well going to see something on this trip besides the insides of tavernas.

An hour more into her trek, she passed a pair of girls herding a desultory tribe of goats along the roadside. Mira stopped and asked, in her limited Greek, what there might be of interest up ahead. The girls shared that look of dull slow-wittedness that Mira had come to recognize as characteristic of Kirinos's inhabitants, a vacuity that suggested spirits no less desolate than the barren landscape.

The two girls conversed in low whispers before one said, in Greek the gist of which Mira was able to comprehend, "There's the ruin of a temple close by, but you don't want to go there. It isn't safe."

"It's been abandoned for a long time," the other said.

"A temple to the goddess Baubo," said the first.

"Baubo?" Mira repeated, unfamiliar with the name.

A faint trace of slyness leaked into the first speaker's large and bovine eyes, the closest thing to an expression of amusement that Mira had seen since coming to the island.

Mira wanted to question the women further, but the goats were straying, the girls obviously impatient to be on their way. Mira thanked them, hoping she had understood correctly, and pedaled on.

A few miles farther on, she walked her decrepit bike (no less ancient, however, than her legs were beginning to feel) up a steep hill topped by stands of poplars. Wind-flogged for their entire lives, the trees were permanently bent before their batterer, slanting out of the loose and rocky soil like broken bones set by a sadist, all weird twists and angles.

But for the grotesquely warped trees, the hilltop appeared as forlorn and barren as the rest of Kirinos, abandoned even by the wind today, but for a sluggish breeze.

And Baubo's temple? If it existed at all (and Mira was beginning to imagine that she'd been sent on a wild-goose chase reserved for the most gullible of tourists—a Greek snipe hunt, as it were), it must be on still higher ground, well beyond the capacity of both her bike and calf muscles.

Still, the idea of coming back from her day's excursion with not even a small discovery or adventure to recount was incentive enough for Mira to make one final assault on the hilltop. Leaning her bike against a tree, she forced herself on foot up a rock-strewn incline that offered, to mountain goats perhaps, a facsimile of a path.

She reached the top panting, legs atremble.

And halted, disappointment smiting her like a blow across the cheek.

The temple, if that was what it once had been, was now a crumbled relic, defiled by weeds and shat upon by birds. Small lizards sunned themselves on its chipped stones and scurried into shaded cracks at Mira's approach. Only two half-columns yet remained—the rest were tumbled over, sections scattered here and there in what looked, to Mira, like the vertebrae of some long-dead dinosaur, huge cousin perhaps to the toy-sized ones now baking on the stones. The decay and desolation of the place was both disturbing and, somehow also, morbidly alluring. Mira had seen fallen temples before, of course, but either in museums, their bleached stones carefully divided up and labeled, or cordoned off and renovated for display, tramped across by infestations of noisy, camera-snapping tourists.

This was something else. This ruin was deserted, empty, private as a tomb. A tumbled wreck, it well might be, but for the moment, it apparently belonged entirely to Mira. And if the temple was less than she had hoped for, the view from her high perch was stunning, the first vista Mira had found worth setting eyes on. From this vantage point, the sea was so bright it seared spangles on her retinas, each wave composed of a treasure trove of individual gems—turquoise, topaz, and emeralds in a seething jewel box of light.

Clambering over a row of fallen stones, Mira unhooked her daypack and sank down onto the ground. She spread her lunch out around her—a canteen of ice water, now tepid slush, granola bars purchased in Athens, grapes and pears from the kiosk outside the hotel.

A breeze nipped and flitted at the damp hair on the back of her neck. She sank her teeth into a pear, its nectar overflowing her lips and dribbling down her chin, and thought of C.J. back at the taverna, probably chatting up Greek girls and maybe boys as well, if she'd imbibed enough retsina.

But maybe, Mira thought, *C.J. had the right idea. At least she's never lonely, isn't eating her lunch right now at the bitter end of nowhere without even goats for company.*

The breeze picked up a bit, moaning plaintively through stunted tree limbs.

It died off, but the moaning didn't. The sound continued unabated and took on, in fact, a distinctly human timbre.

Mira froze, unsure of what to do. To pursue the sound might invite involvement in some drama in which Mira, as a foreigner and tourist, could ill afford to embroil herself. Neither was it clear to her if the sounds were fathered by great pain or by pleasure. If the former, then decency demanded she investigate. There could be a hiker hurt, a young child lost, even an injured animal, although more and more, Mira doubted that the noise could have any except human origin.

She crept forward as quietly as her bulk allowed, scuttling the last yard or two on hands and knees, and peered between some scrubby bushes.

At first glance, she saw but didn't really *see,* so improbable was the spectacle before her that she assumed her vision must be playing tricks, creating the illusion that a trio of the bleached and fallen stones were now a woman's round thighs and ivory belly.

No hallucination this, however, Mira realized; the flush and jiggle of abundant flesh was all too real.

A woman, endowed with Junoesque proportions, lay spread out upon the rough ground. Her knees were bent, thigh's widely V'd. With three fingers of her right hand, she rhythmically fucked herself, while with the left she parted the pink creases of her labia, plucking at the engorged clitoris with her thumb. Though she lay in shadow, sunlight broke through in places, dappling her flesh with spots and splashes the color of buttered Brie. With each thrust of her fingers, the woman moaned and arched her back, black tresses tumbling over the earth like so many writhing serpents. Sweat rolled off her mounded breasts and belly, shimmered on her nipple tips like opals.

Mira knew she had no business witnessing this display and yet she couldn't bring herself to look away. She gazed on, rapt, and was still staring, fingers of one hand lightly touching her own bosom, tweaking at a nipple, when the woman's eyes suddenly flashed open and she looked directly at the spot where Mira crouched.

Her eyes held the force of twin beacons. Mira cringed before their power, determined to keep silent, but the very underbrush was bent upon betraying her. A twig snapped beneath her shifting weight; a stone, dislodged by her heel, went skittering.

"Who's there?" the woman called out in Greek.

Mira's head thundered with blood.

"I'm sorry," she blurted out. "I'm going."

"Wait."

Mira halted, bracing herself for a lambasting the individual words of which she might not comprehend, but whose meaning would be all too clear as well as justified.

The woman, who'd made no attempt to cover herself and whose garments, Mira noted, were nowhere in view, stood up and approached her. And kept approaching, past that invisible boundary which varies with each culture, but whose limits with regard to personal space are normally respected.

"Pedhi mou," my girl, whispered the woman and put her mouth to Mira's.

Her kiss was hot and salty, tasting of sweat and sex and female juices. It was, thought Mira, like giving head to a woman in the final stages of arousal, the pussy dripping with desire, the vulval lips engorged and oozing sex.

This is madness, she thought, and yet her lips were parting to allow access to her mouth and she was unresistant when the woman began to unbutton and peel off her blouse and shorts, her sweat-drenched undergarments. Mira's large breasts were squashed against a bosom far more abundant that her own. Her head spun with the folly of her own lust, with a passion so unnatural to her character that she felt at once transformed and yet possessed, as though surely something outside herself inspired this abandon.

The woman's body, lush and hot, bumped and rutted against Mira's. Fingers probed and parted her, a tongue both skilled and playful teased her lips and lashes, then ducked down to drink from the tiny cup of sweat that was her navel.

And all the while the woman made noises—sucking, gobbling, slurping, laughing—as their bodies thumped and squeaked together in a carnal melody. The woman guided Mira to the ground onto a bed made of her discarded clothing. Her avid lips sought out the mouth between Mira's parted legs, where she drank of sweat and cunt juice. Mira thrashed and cried out as an orgasm shuddered through her, contractions like a birth of pleasure throbbing all the way into her womb. The woman's tongue explored new crevices and creases. More climaxes were wrung from her, the last of these so violent that Mira locked her thighs together and cried out for a respite.

Her lover, however, suffered no such loss of appetite. Leaving Mira on the ground, she pranced and strutted like an obscene jester, tweaking brown nipples the size of coffee saucers, strumming at her clitoris with the fast and fluid motions of a virtuoso guitarist. Muttering some words that Mira didn't understand, she squatted over the rough earth, reached down and spread herself wide in a parody of childbirth. Astonished, Mira watched this spectacle, unsure if this outrageous lewdness was prelude to some new bout of lovemaking. Her nether lips still throbbed and tingled from the force of her last orgasm. She felt undone, sapped senseless by the heat and the intensity of sex. She had neither the strength nor will to do anything but recline and watch the dance.

Which turned suddenly, before Mira's bewitched gaze, into a monstrous birthing. The woman spread her thick thighs wide, parting vaginal lips that hung down more than an inch below the black thatch of pubic hair. She released a gust of laughter that stirred the still air and raised the hair on Mira's arms with it's dark mirth.

Something slick and shiny glistened wetly at the lips of her vagina. The thing pulsed there for an instant, like the damp head of a grotesquely misshapen child, then fell to the rough ground, where it uncoiled powerful hind legs and leaped away.

Mira gaped, unable to comprehend what she had seen, but the miracle was only just commencing. The woman was giving birth to toads, hordes of the wet and mottled creatures dropping from her cunt, a slithering rain of amphibian life upon the stones. Born full grown, they leaped in all directions, a sea of bright, bulging eyes and livid mouths.

Mira gasped and clutched both hands across her breasts, although they offered scant protection against the unnatural hordes that were still plopping, like dollops of green dung, from the woman's cunt.

A toad leaped at Mira's face and landed in her hair. Another bounced across her belly, a third's passing marked her breast with smears of dirt from its webbed hind feet.

Mira screamed and writhed, dislodging the toads on her legs and head only to find three more arranged like horrid tumors upon her breasts and belly. The largest of these, endowed with shining amber eyes, seized the soft flesh below Mira's navel and delivered a painful bite. Blood slicked the toad's wide mouth, and bile rose up in Mira's throat. The world turned. She tried to rise but found her limbs were powerless, her vision growing inky at the edges.

Through a gauze of sick terror, she could still see the horrid birthing taking place. As she passed out, her ears rang with the woman's mad laughter that almost—but not completely—drowned out a sound far worse, the soft, throaty glugging of the toads.

"You shouldn't have gone out in the heat today," C.J. said, nibbling at a piece of fried octopus. "You look like hell."

"I'm all right," said Mira, cutting into the leg of lamb the waiter had just set before her. "Just hungry."

Hungry and—if truth be known—bizarrely energized. Her belly throbbed, but not with pain. More like concentric circles of appetite and energy radiating out from the wound on her stomach. The toad appeared to have nipped out a tiny chunk of flesh. The bleeding had been copious on her bike ride back to town. Mira had been forced to hurry back to the hotel, where she had shed her filthy clothing and stuffed it deep inside her duffle bag.

Fortunately, other than remarking on Mira's appearance, C.J. had shown little curiosity about her day. Now she added some more water to her glass of ouzo and sipped the milky liquid with that look of studied smugness that Mira had come to recognize as presaging some admission aimed at provoking jealousy.

"I met someone today. His name's Stavros. He grew up here, but he worked in his cousin's restaurant in New York for a couple of years, so he speaks really good English."

Mira shrugged and forked a chunk of meat into her mouth. "So did you fuck him yet?"

C.J. recoiled. "No, of course not. I'm with you, aren't I?"

"I don't know. Are you?"

"Jesus, we're in a pissy mood tonight."

"So what's the point of telling me about some guy you met? To make me jealous, right? To remind me how fucking desirable you are to each and every gender. Well, fuck him if you want to. Suck his dick until it falls off. I don't care."

"God, Mira, what's got into you? I only said…"

"This looks so good," said Mira, reaching over with her fork to poke at C.J.'s food. She chose the longest piece of octopus, a tentacle pale and tender as the flesh of an armpit, studded with small, rose-colored suckers.

C.J., misunderstanding her intention, said, "I thought you didn't like octopus. You said it was disgusting."

"I didn't say I was going to eat it." Mira plucked the tentacle from the fork and held it between her fingers. "Look here."

She glanced to either side of her. Only a few of the tables in the taverna were filled and these by locals whose faces, in most cases, were either directed at their plates or wreathed in a fog of cigarette smoke. Slowly, savoring C.J.'s agitation, she undid the top three buttons of her blouse, revealing ample cleavage unfettered by a bra.

"I wonder if your friend Stavros would like to do this with his tongue?" She slid the octopus between her freckled breasts. Up and down, down and up, leaving a sheen of grease against the pale skin.

"Jesus, Mira, stop it."

"But then your tits are smaller than mine, so he might rather tonguefuck you other places."

She slid sideways in her chair, pulled her cotton skirt up to mid-thigh. She wore no underpants, and her cunt was moist and ready. On the first push, the tentacle got away from her and slid so far inside, she almost lost it. Mira threw back her head and howled with laughter at the thought of walking around being fucked with an octopus dildo inside her, but then her vaginal muscles clenched and pushed the slippery stob back out. It slithered into her fingers.

"Mira, *please,* the waiter's coming over."

"You think he'd like to watch?"

She closed her legs and pulled down her skirt, but didn't bother to refasten the buttons of her blouse.

"For God's sake…"

Mira grinned. She put the octopus tentacle between her lips and began to gobble it with noisy, smacking sounds.

"You're fucking drunk."

"I've had half a glass of wine."

"Close up your blouse. Your tits are falling out."

Mira giggled and undid another button, revealing small pink nipples that were celebrating their exposure with exuberant erections. She felt appalled at her audacity, astonished, and yet elated, too. There was merit, more profound than her mind could shape at present, in this loss of dignity and decorum, but if so, C.J. was blind to it. She gaped in horror at her lover as the waiter, unable to contain himself, came over and stared down at Mira's chest.

His eyes bugged, and he muttered something that Mira didn't understand. Others had turned to stare now, diners abandoning their meals to ogle the impromptu cabaret act.

"Please," said C.J., through gritted teeth. "I don't know what you're trying to prove, but cover yourself up."

Mira stuck out her tongue at C.J., waggled it around, and slowly, so slowly that the act of covering herself became more seductive than the original unveiling, began to close the buttons.

The diners, murmuring now among themselves, continued to stare, looking from Mira to one another and back to Mira again with an expression more of wonder than disapproval.

A muscular young man with blindingly white teeth, evidently C.J.'s new Greek swain, approached the table with a hand held out to greet his American friend. His eyes were fixed on C.J. until, at the last moment, his gaze took a sudden detour onto Mira's semi-naked breasts. He gulped, Adam's apple bobbing in his throat, and blushed bright crimson. Murmuring something in Greek, he backed away from the table as though the barrels of two .45's had suddenly been trained on him.

"Stavros," C.J. called out. "Stavros, wait." She pulled a fistful of drachmas out of her pocket and slammed them onto the table. "Come on, Mira. If you're not drunk, then you're high or sick or something. I've got to get you out of here before you cause a riot."

And, at least in part, Mira agreed with her. Yet if, indeed, she'd somehow tripped or blundered over the edge of insanity, then surely this was an experience far more pleasurable than her previous, albeit limited, study of mental deviations (mostly undergraduate psych courses) would have led her to believe.

She felt, indeed, more energetic than she had in years, infused with a heat so galvanizing that, as C.J. half dragged her along the street, Mira thought surely she must be radiating light.

"Where are we going?" she laughed.

"Back to the room. Where you can sober up."

"But I *am* sober." Mira tried to stop giggling for C.J.'s sake, but with every effort to compose herself, the laughter only burst from her in more lusty gales. "More sober than I've ever been."

"Then you're having some kind of breakdown. Heat prostration maybe."

They passed a group of men. "Wait," cried Mira. Pulling free of C.J.'s grasp, she bent over, flipped her skirt up, and wagged her naked rump at the startled passersby. This small act seemed insufficient, however, to encompass her frivolity. Reaching back, she spread her cheeks, exposing the pink and puckered eyelet at her center.

The men stopped in their tracks.

"Mira!"

C.J. yanked the skirt down. With her right hand, she cracked Mira a resounding blow across the face. "Do you want to get us both arrested? Thrown in a fucking Greek jail?"

"Fucking Greek jail?" echoed Mira. She rubbed her stung cheek. Her face hurt, but something else, something altogether wonderful and unexpected, was distracting her from the pain. From the nearby plaza: music. The first music Mira had heard since they arrived on this godforsaken lump of rock. A lyre, sweet and lyrical, and joining it, the chimelike notes of a *laouto*.

"Fucking Greek jail!" sang out Mira and she began to dance.

Her legs, despite this morning's trek, were suddenly featherlight. She was a bird, a bawd, a buxom ballerina. She was great, unholstered, jiggly tits and quivering fat ass and a canyon of cleavage. She was madness, mirth, and celebration.

"Mira! No! If you don't stop this instant, I'm leaving!"

"Then go!" cried Mira and danced away.

Her sandals slapped the cobblestones. Leather on stone, fuck, fuck, like lusty mating. Mira laughed and kicked them off. She whirled and capered, spun and leaped, and the musicians picked up the beat and Mira danced, and did her blouse fall open of its own accord or did her fingers tease the buttons free? She didn't know, but somehow her tits flopped out, and the musicians yodeled at the sky like moonstruck hounds and then the moon itself swelled from behind the clouds in all its naked splendor and Mira sang out, "Fucking Greek jail!" and danced and danced.

A few villagers gathered round to stare and grunt, before retreating, like shamed wraiths, back into their houses, white as bone shards beneath the yellow moon.

And the musicians' energy waned, and they put away their instruments and slunk away, but still Mira cavorted, her white skirt swirling, pink nipples dancing their own jig and she was like a Catherine wheel, all light and glamour, spinning wildly in the dark.

A boy, barely beyond his teens, watched her with a rapt and avid gaze, wetting the corners of his mouth with a tongue made sopping by desire. Mira danced to his side. She took him by his thick black hair and buried his face between her breasts, each one of which was easily the size of the boy's head. She let him suckle, leaving her nipples silvery with saliva, then pushed his head down and hoisted up her skirt and straddled him. His tongue knew dances of its own, quick, darting strumming motions and deep, luxurious slurps and she opened up her folds to him and took his tongue in like a raw pink fetus seeking reentry to its fleshy nest.

The boy stood up and unzipped himself, took out a bobbing, uncut cock. The sight of it made Mira giggle with delight and recommence her dance, though the music to which she capered was now within her head.

An old man rushed out from a nearby doorway. He grabbed the boy and shouted in his face with much agitation. Mira heard the word "Baubo," but didn't understand the rest. Beneath the elder's scorn, the boy shrank both literally and figuratively. He slunk away, the old man's arm prodding him roughly along. Leaving Mira panting, bare-breasted, and alone in the center of the plaza. She looked down at herself and gasped, began buttoning her blouse. Wetness ran between her legs, the boy's drool and her own juices. From her groin and armpits wafted, unmistakably, the pungency of lust.

The door was locked when Mira at last returned to the hotel room. She knocked and pleaded a good long time before C.J. let her in. C.J.'s tanned face was tracked with angry tears.

"I talked to Stavros. Tomorrow morning, he's leaving on the first ferry back to Piraeus," said C.J., crawling back into bed. "I'm going with him. I want you to come with us. We'll find a doctor for you in Athens. An English-speaking one."

Mira took off her soiled and rumpled clothing and slid naked into bed next to her lover.

"I can't do that," she said. "I don't understand what happened out there, but, oh God, it felt so wonderful."

"When you exposed yourself, you mean. When you mooned those men."

"Yes, wonderful," said Mira, her voice awed and tiny. "I don't understand. It was like I couldn't stop myself. And I didn't want to."

"You're lucky you weren't beaten up or arrested. These people are conservative. They aren't used to things like this. Did you see the way they looked at you?"

"What's happening to me, C.J.? Am I crazy?"

"I don't know. Maybe you had some kind of fit. Maybe some blood sugar thing. But Stavros thinks it's..."

"Yeah? What does pretty little Stavros think?"

C.J.'s voice became so tiny Mira could barely hear her. "This sounds crazy, but...he says this island used to be dedicated to the worship of a deity named Balbo or Baubo or something. Anyway, she's the goddess of obscenity, of lewdness and sensuality. And he thinks...oh, forget it..."

"He thinks that I'm possessed. That's it, isn't it? That's why he wants to leave. Before whatever I've got gets spread around."

"Look, I'm sorry I said anything. It's nonsense, silly superstition. Stavros isn't educated. He still believes the old Greek myths and legends."

Mira looked at the smooth wall of C.J.'s back, remembering the woman at the temple, her kisses like honeyed darts, both sweet and penetrating. She wanted to tell C.J. what had happened, everything, but she knew that would be impossible. C.J. wouldn't understand. She'd only be more convinced that Stavros was a beautiful but superstitious rube and Mira was simply crazy.

"You have to leave here tomorrow when Stavros and I go," said C.J.

"Your new lover."

"I didn't say that."

"But he will be."

"Maybe."

Mira thought about it briefly. "Go fuck yourself."

Daylight splashed across Mira's sleeping face like hot liquid. She gasped and clutched the pillow. A warm breeze gusted in the open window where sunbeams streamed in to form an avenue of light.

C.J. was gone, the only evidence that she had ever been there the indentation of her head still on the pillow.

Mira got up and began to dress. The wound on her belly twinged. She looked down past her swollen breasts and saw that it was still open, a tiny bud-red slit below her navel. She touched it lightly with one finger and almost had an orgasm. Pleasure swam through her, stem to stern. Her head spun with the delirium of last night's ecstasy as she made her way outside into the village.

She had considered her few options and made a decision: She would go back to Baubo's temple and see if she could find some clue, or better yet, some respite from the madness that had overtaken her. That, at least, was her rationale. In truth, she hoped to find her lover of the day before, the goddess who gave birth to frogs and, perhaps more frighteningly, had incited her to last night's wantonness.

The day was furious with heat, the breeze offering no respite except to stir and redistribute the torpor as Mira started up the dirt track to the temple. No one was about. The village seemed deserted, even the taverna on the waterfront bereft of its usual clientele of domino-playing males. She moved slowly, her body stiff and achy from last night's outlandish exercise. At a crest in the journey, she paused to look out over the water and saw a large boat, a ferry, plowing westward in the direction of Piraeus.

Her heart caught and hitched as though a claw had punctured her aorta—C.J. and her new toy Stavros were surely on that boat.

Something moved on the horizon in the corner of her vision. She gazed behind her and staggered backward. Running, stumbling up the dirt track, came a dozen or more villagers. The man in the lead looked up and saw Mira. He pointed, beckoned to the others, urging them on. They began to run in earnest.

Mira stumbled forward in blind panic. So C.J. had been right—last night's escapades were not so easily forgotten or forgiven. Perhaps she would be jailed or expelled from the country. Or worse—something in the villagers' pursuit put her in mind of fates more ancient and punitive—adulteresses stoned and wanton women entombed alive in cloister walls.

She began to run, thinking only that she must reach the temple, that Baubo—witch, goddess, whatever she might be—might help her, offer her a place to hide.

Her limbs were flagging, but terror lent her strength. She cut through fields of olive trees, skirting the sea, and climbed at last to the crest of the final bluff where the madwoman had given birth to toads.

And stopped, the breath rasping in her chest, unable to summon even one last reserve for further flight.

They were waiting for her. Hundreds of them. The entire village. They had known that she would come here and had arrived first, leaving only a handful behind to goad her into flight.

"Please," said Mira, but she knew the word was meaningless. They had not gone to all this trouble to merely turn away and leave her to her madness.

She took a few halting steps. The villagers stared.

Someone pulled out a dulcimer and began a melody. Another blew into a primitive bagpipe, the *tsambouna*.

The music threaded through the silence like a golden needle passing through white cotton.

Laughter started.

Mira didn't realize until some moments later that the weird, manic laughter was produced by her own throat, but its effect was instantaneous. The villagers began to jerk and twitch in what, at first glance, appeared to Mira to be a crude dance but which was, in actuality, a clumsy striptease. They began to caper and leap about, flinging items of their clothing into the air. Their aimless exuberance reminded Mira of the frogs' mad leaping, except that now the random jumping was accompanied by a hundred small obscenities.

A young woman with a baby on her hip exposed large rosy-nippled breasts. She squeezed and twisted a breast and milk squirted forth. It struck the face of a dancing man who opened his mouth wide and gobbled. Others gathered round. The woman emptied both breasts into the throng, milk running in hair and eyes, dripping from smacking lips.

Old women clad in widow's black scattered their funereal garb across the temple stones. Cackling, they caressed themselves and capered in lewd jigs.

An old man bent over and let loose a hornpipe melody of exuberant flatulence. The rhythm of his obscene tooting kept time with the *tsambouna* and the dulcimer while others laughed and clapped.

A woman lifted up her breast and suckled from her own nipple while with her other hand she milked the semen from the penis of her partner. A dog joined in the fray, aroused and thrusting at the dancers' legs. Some women dropped onto their hands and knees and vied to suck the canine's crimson stalk.

And madder grew the dancers and wilder their excesses with flowers plucked to make bouquets protruding out of anuses and cocks garlanded with spring anemones and vaginas sprouting orchids and rockroses.

The celebrants grabbed Mira by her hands and breasts and buttocks. Their feverish caresses stripped her clothes away and she was swept into the orgy. They peppered her with kisses but reserved the most ardent tonguings for the wound upon her belly, where Baubo's kiss had left a puckered replica of a tiny cunt.

"Baubo has returned to us," some of the old ones murmured. "Baubo has a priestess now, and we can dance again."

In the evening, before returning to the village, they brought Mira jugs of wine and beer and platters of the finest food. The women cleared the earth and made a bed for her amid the ruins of the temple. In the growing dark, alone now, she squatted naked on the hillside, gazing out to sea, trying to remember what was lost to her.

There had been a life for her out there once, school and home and lover, but all that seemed pale and vapid now, dim and distant as the far-off stars and moving rapidly away from her. She let it go with a sense more of relief than loss.

In the night, when she awoke in brief confusion, with fear plucking at her like the beak of some flesh-eating bird, she had only to touch her belly wound and pleasure spiraled up her spine. Her body bloomed with orgasms and her heart with song.

Flamethrower

The idea to blind Cash McCauley during a nontitle match in McCauley's hometown was the brainchild of the head promoter.

Otherwise, Pete Duggan, aka the Servant of Satan, would never have gone for the deal. He was a wrestler, for Christ's sake, not a magician. Dropkicks and atom smashers were his forte, not sleight of hand. Making a "fireball" appear to roll from his arm into McCauley's face was an illusion he'd spent the better part of a week perfecting. And McCauley—well, as usual the babyface got the easy work—all he had to do was clutch his eyes, scream bloody Jesus, and tumble outside the ring, where Duggan would proceed to stomp and punch and gouge him till it looked like somebody'd emptied a bottle of Heinz 57 over the kid's head.

Taped and replayed on about forty affiliate stations nation-wide, the match would set the climate for the real moneymak-er, a climactic confrontation several weeks away when McCauley, his sight miraculously restored, would face Duggan for the Global Wrestling world title in Madison Square Garden.

Now, poised on top of the turnbuckle, getting ready to launch his 260-pound bulk onto McCauley's prone form, the Prince of Hell's Servant looked satanic indeed. An "X" was shaved into his chest hair, extending from hirsute pecs down to a modest roll of fat at the top of his trunks. A crimson pen-tagram decorated his forehead, and black slashes, more like Indian warpaint than satanic adornment, bisected his face cheek to jowl. His black hair was scraped back in a ponytail, giv-ing him the overall appearance of Charlie Manson beefed up on steroids.

In short, business as usual. Pete Duggan's work might lack dignity but it brought him close to half a million a year, plus some dynamite perks in the pussy department. One of them, with lush tits packed into a black halter top and jeans so tight they outlined the "V" of her cunt, was waiting backstage for him right now. Duggan could hardly wait to finish this show, so he could get on to the next one.

Meantime, the fans were going out of their fucking minds. In the Percy High School auditorium, where McCauley had fin-ished school eight years ago, bedlam reigned. People hurled debris at Duggan—spitballs, hairpins, half-full cans of beer. A young kid, bolder or dumber than most, raced past to try to grind a lighted cigarette into Duggan's thigh, but the move was too late—Duggan had already launched himself from the turn-buckle and was in the air, crashing onto McCauley's splayed body, while the referee yelled for the bell.

Cash McCauley, ever the hero, battled back. Duggan let him get in a few token blows before he reared back and launched what the promoter promised would make him the most notorious and highest-earning villain in Global Wrestling history: the Fireball.

The brief explosion of smoke and sparks was actually the result of a flashpot concealed in a turnbuckle and triggered off-stage by the black Superstar, Hacksaw Ames, but what the fans saw was McCauley recoiling in pain before crashing head first onto the concrete floor. Blood spurted from McCauley's split head as he screamed, "Help me, I'm blind!" and collapsed in a twitching, gore-splattered heap.

Some fans looked enraged enough to attack Duggan them-selves, but McCauley's cries were the cue for Hacksaw Ames and Killer Duke Savage to come charging to the rescue. They fended off Duggan, then hoisted McCauley between them and carted the fallen good guy backstage.

"Hail Satan!" roared Duggan as the fans tried to overpower his hated voice with catcalls of rage. "Hail Satan, Lord of the Universe!"

Moments later, a contingent of cops escorted Duggan through the mob toward the dressing rooms. Duggan felt good. The little choreographed dance with McCauley had gotten his adren-alin rushing. He felt like a Hun galloping over the steppes with a captive virgin strapped to his saddle or a Viking getting ready to ravage the women of an enemy town. He was pumped up with testosterone and ready to rut.

With his dick already at half-mast just thinking about her, he hoped Carlie hadn't gotten impatient and gone off with some other wrestler. She was new to the ringrat scene. Hacksaw Ames, who'd tried unsuccessfully to get a blowjob from her the week before in the Denver Coliseum, said she'd expressed a prefer-ence for heels. Most of the ringrats were partial to babyfaces, young studs like McCauley, who had the face of a junior choir-boy but, in Duggan's view, was kinkier than a carload of queers. Occasionally, though, you found a girl who only screwed heels, who got wet for wrestling's mad dogs and psychos and servants of Satan. In Duggan's experience, they were the wildest of all. He needn't have worried about the post-match entertainment. She was there waiting for him, a kind of cowgirl version of the perfect wet dream. Oval face framed in abundant layers of shaggy, bleached hair, plump, bitten-looking lips that begged to be penetrated, tits so big underneath the gaudy Western shirt that Duggan expected sequins to start popping off at any moment. She stood on one foot, the other braced against the wall behind her, fringe dangling from her silver-buckled cowboy boots. Her eyes, he noticed, were a little weird, slitty and slutty-looking, Madonna on ludes. Like a woman who's been knocked around too much or popped more downers than a sugar freak with a bag of M&M's.

Either way, Duggan didn't give a shit. Whether punch-drunk or stoned, her bland, rather bovine expression suggested a submissiveness and willingness to please, even to be humiliated, that he found powerfully arousing.

Too arousing to head for the motel, in fact, before getting a little taste.

He draped an arm around her, dangling a beefy hand inside her cleavage. Her tits were fucking amazing, like silk-wrapped honeydews. "You enjoy the match, darlin'?"

"It was hot. Especially the ending. I just wish you could've thrown more fire. If you had…"

"All in a night's work," Duggan said, not really listening. His fingers found a jutting nipple, tweaked it hard enough to hurt. She gave an appreciative shudder. "You gonna be good to ol' Duggan tonight?"

"Real good." Her eyes were slitted down so narrow he couldn't see the color of the irises. Her voice was as husky as if she'd gargled with cum. Duggan's steadily engorging dick was testing the limits of his jockstrap. Quickly, he ushered Carlie into a small, private dressing area with a massage table and some lockers.

"Come on, I want a preliminary match before we go to the motel."

He set her on the massage table and opened up the gaudy sequined blouse, undid the frontal clasp on her red brassiere, letting her breasts loll forth in D-cup opulence. Her cleavage released a musky heat. He buried his face there, breathing the steamy, not-quite-clean scent of her.

Then he was unbuckling her belt and yanking down her jeans to reveal, beneath the scarlet satin underpants, a pussy redolent of sex and meaty lips pierced in three places by heavy, clinking cunt rings. The gleaming rings, the sound and shine of them, made Duggan want to fuck her all the more, but her jeans were rolled down around her boots. He couldn't get her legs open.

"Take them things off."

She hesitated.

"Take it all off, so I can spread ya."

She bent forward and tugged off her right boot, then paused before removing the left one.

Duggan noticed it now—the disparity in boot size. The right one was a normal boot, the left was built up by an inch or more and broader toward the toe. The fringe worked to some extent as camouflage, but up close the oddity of shape was obvious.

"Look, I'd rather keep this on."

But Duggan's dick and curiosity were both up now. He grabbed the boot and yanked it off. The sock went, too. He stared.

Christ, she's fucking deformed. That was his first thought. Then: *McCauley'd come for this. He's into freaks. Hey, what the fuck. She ain't so perfect as I thought. I ought to share.*

The left foot was a mangled wreck, four toes fused into a kind of club, the big toe just a nailless nub, pink and sickeningly fetal-looking. There was no arch and the heel looked almost peeled away, chopped cheese.

"You in an accident or somethin'?"

Her head and tits all shook: three "nos."

"I've always been this way." She shrugged, then V'd her thighs, offering wet lips almost as scarlet as the lipsticked ones above. Duggan pushed her back onto the table, kicked off his sweaty wrestling trunks and thrust inside. Her pussy muscles closed around him like a greased fist. On the in stroke, the metal rings rubbed against his balls, on the out stroke they clanked like tribal music. He hoisted up her legs and pounded deep, almost straight down, hands kneading those enormous boobs, his weight flattening them against her chest, thumbing turgid nipples.

The violence with which he fucked usually made women scream with pain or passion, but though her body arched and writhed in all the expected ways, Carlie's face betrayed no trace of feeling. The crimson mouth stayed slack and parted, the eyes were as vacant of response as mirrored glasses. She seemed to be adrift within some inner world—a private fantasy perhaps, or visions of another lover, some setting more exotic or romantic than a narrow dressing room and the massage table with its repellent Rorschachs of bodily secretions.

Duggan slid out and mashed her tits together while he fucked her cleavage. She lifted her head, tongue wagging, and slicked his cockhead with saliva until they were connected in yet another way, a glistening string of spit joining dick and lower lip. He watched her fixing on his cock with that blank, bewitched gaze, eyes almost shut but staring, taking aim with her quick tongue like a transfixed snake. Not once did she look at Duggan's face. Just his cockhead, sliding out between her breasts, like the bald head of a baby emerging from a veined and meaty birth canal.

When he came, cum spewed across her sulky face, a milky torrent festooning teased and brittle locks and clinging to her lashes.

Her lush body lay beneath him like an expanse of gorgeous dunes and beach. Reluctantly, Duggan rolled off her. He watched as she hurriedly pulled up her jeans and yanked the built-up boot over her deformed foot.

McCauley was going to love this one. Maybe Hacksaw, too. In the business, it never hurt to do a favor here and there and, now that he'd discovered her imperfection, Duggan was eager that the others have her, too.

"That was just a warm-up," he told Carlie. "You run around to the East entrance and wait for me. We'll find ourselves a nice motel and do this all night long."

She gave him a quick, sly smile, the closest thing to an expression of emotion that Duggan had seen all evening.

"You don't mind about my foot?"

"No, darlin', that don't bother me. Fact is, it kinda makes you special."

Kinda makes me want to puke, he thought, but canceled out the image by focusing on the rest of her: prime cut.

Back in the dressing room, Duggan quickly rounded up

McCauley and Hacksaw Ames and told them about the sweet piece of ass with the huge tits and freak-show foot. Hacksaw, who wasn't keen on deformities, had to be convinced, but McCauley had a taste for the bizarre (he claimed to have once fucked a woman with both legs amputated at the thighs) and wouldn't have cared if the girl had had an extra head once Duggan described what her foot looked like. Duggan told the other two wrestlers where to meet him, then quickly showered and dressed.

A security guard was stationed at the rear exit when Duggan was ready to leave. Duggan approached him. "Have the animals gone home yet, or they still hanging around?"

The guard was young, gawky as a grasshopper, with an Adam's apple the size of a plum yo-yoing in his throat and a tag pinned to his chest that said *Wally*. Duggan could have lifted him over his head and flung him away like a javelin.

"Just your typical lynch mob," the guard said amiably. "I wouldn't worry too much. Only a few got shotguns."

Duggan didn't smile. Security was one thing he didn't joke about. Just last month, a well-known heel had gotten acid flung in his face as he was leaving the Richmond Coliseum.

"Mine's the '93 Corvette," said Duggan, jangling keys wrapped in a five-dollar bill. "Drive it around to the East entrance. Lady's waitin' for me there, just inside the door."

The guard glanced outside at the hangers-on. A small cross dangled inside his open shirt collar, and he fingered it nervously as he watched the angry crowd gathered there. "You better not plan on staying in Percy tonight, Mr. Duggan. Some of these guys spot your car, you'll wish you'd drove here in a tank."

"Most of 'em are so drunk they'll be lucky to find their own cars, assuming they got one," Duggan snorted. He couldn't resist adding, "I know a motel out toward Mooreville, way back off the road. Got mirrors on the ceiling, dirty movies on the TV. Lots of privacy."

He leered, enjoying the kid's obvious envy as he went off to fetch Duggan's car.

Tonight had been two of Duggan's best performances—the public show and the private one—and the hottest of the night's entertainment hadn't even begun yet.

Minutes later, at the rear door of the auditorium, Duggan changed places with the security guard in the driver's seat of the Vette and turned to plant a quick kiss on Carlie's mouth, which was painted with lipstick so close in color to blood-red that for a second, as Duggan's face approached hers, her mouth looked like an open, bleeding wound.

But their mouths never made contact.

Behind the car, somebody yelled, "There's the son-of-a-bitch! Get him!" Something smashed into the Corvette's roof, something else hit a door. A howl went up like that of a wolf pack surrounding a deer.

"Shit!" Duggan glanced in the rearview mirror and saw a mob of about two dozen people round the corner of the high school and swoop down on the car. A rock bounced off the Vette's bumper. Suddenly people were grabbing for the door handles, and a florid-faced youth in a black T-shirt was mashing his pimples against the glass, screaming obscenities. Another man flung himself across the hood, making the sign of the cross and spraying the windshield with spittle.

Yelling at Carlie to hang on, Duggan floored the accelerator. The car shot forward and careened into the parking lot. The boy on the hood rolled off. The one hanging onto the door ran alongside for a few seconds, then dropped back.

Duggan cut across the parking lot, veering around the few cars that remained, took a quick right onto Route 11, then a succession of turns onto side streets lined with dark, boxy houses surrounded by shade trees. For a long time he kept an eye on the rearview mirror as he wove a circuitous path out of town.

For now, he seemed to have lost them.

"Christ," he said, glancing at Carlie, who was gnawing that wonderfully plump lower lip, but otherwise looking as emotionless as ever. Duggan tried to make her smile. "Aren't you afraid to be seen with me? These Bible thumpers don't have much of a sense of humor when it comes to Satan."

"Assholes," she snorted with surprising venom. "Redneck trash. Too bad you can't use your fireball. Shoot fire down their throats till they shit cinders."

It was an unexpected image, one that made Duggan laugh.

"What was it you said before, darlin'? About making the fire-ball bigger or something?"

"Yeah, bigger. Like you do other things." Her hand roamed his inner leg, moved higher, expertly exploring. "You know, you got guts claiming to be in cahoots with old Lucifer. You ain't scared, taking the Devil's name in vain to liven up your show?"

Duggan laughed. "Reckon if there is a Devil, he's the one ought to be worrying about me. Like when I get to hell, I just might organize an overthrow and run the place myself."

Carlie gave him a cat-eyed stare. "Duggan, you are one cocky bastard."

They drove in silence for a while, turning onto a two-lane road that wound through a hilly, wooded area, past the bleak-looking Percy Juvenile Correctional Center, an out-of-business convenience store, and a veterinary clinic. When they passed a bar advertising "NUDES! LIVE!" Duggan made a joke about some bars offering dead ones, and Carlie laughed with the hot, contented pleasure he'd seen on women right after they'd gotten or given really great head.

It was a teasing, mirthful sound, the notes of which went straight to his crotch. She reached over and unzipped him, let his cock pop free. While Duggan drove, she buried her face in his crotch, lapping the head of his dick with the enthusiasm of a child for a particularly delicious ice-cream treat. Her tongue made playful curlicues over the slicked bulb, then traced the vein along the shaft until her nose nested in the springy hair around his balls. "Keep goin', darlin'. You got a regular little Hoover there in your throat."

He eased deeper in the seat, floored the accelerator while Carlie deep-throated him like she was about to suck the cum right out of his balls.

They pulled into the parking lot of the Greenway Motel with Carlie's platinum head still pogoing in his lap. McCauley's BMW and Hacksaw's Hertz convertible were already in the lot, parked outside an end room with the lights on and the door ajar. Duggan parked far in the back, hiding the Vette behind a couple of dumpsters.

Just before they got to the door of the motel room, Duggan said to Carlie, "I got a little surprise for you."

"And what would that be?"

He didn't answer but gave the motel door a shove with one hand and pushed Carlie in with the other. She stumbled into the room to the delight of Hacksaw and McCauley, who were watching a late movie and drinking beer.

"Seein' as you like rasslers so good," Duggan said, "how 'bout you show a good time to two of my friends?"

"No. I want it to be just the two of us."

"Yeah, but this is better," said McCauley, getting up from the chair. "You got three holes. Now you got three dicks to go in 'em."

"Forget that shit. I'm outta here."

She wasn't. Not while McCauley had his fist in the top of her platinum mane. He threw her back onto the bed. She bounced twice, and Hacksaw held her down while McCauley went for her clothing. He unbuttoned the shirt and whooped out a rebel yell.

"Goddamn, look at them hooters. As big as volleyballs."

Hacksaw reached down, black fingers kneading plush pink flesh.

"Let's see what we got here," said McCauley as he stripped off boot and sock, revealed the stump of foot. "Hot damn, what happened to you, little gal? Your ma take that Thalidomide-shit before you was born or something?"

She didn't try to struggle, just lay there with her head turned slightly to one side, staring at Duggan, who had locked the motel door and was taking off his pants. Her eyes looked empty, almost rolled up into her head. It gave Duggan the creeps, like the hard drive in her brain had been deleted, like her eyeballs had VACANCY signs. He took his dick out and popped it in her unresisting mouth so he wouldn't have to look at her or watch McCauley fondling that ugly, misshapen cowfoot.

When he'd finished, Hacksaw took over and fucked her tits.

Then McCauley flipped her over and reamed her ass, yanking on her hair like a rodeo rider clinging onto the mane of a bronc while her big boobs flopped and smacked against her chest like udders. Her eyes were shut now, but her lips were parted, slick with spit and cum, so Hacksaw walked around and plugged her face with his nine-incher. They got a rhythm going with the woman's body between them, thrusting back and forth like two men working a bandsaw, and when Hacksaw came, he spewed jism in a long arc that actually spattered the TV screen four feet away.

Afterwards, Duggan flicked on the TV set to CNN Sports, which was repeating highlights from a Redskins game he'd missed the night before and Hacksaw snoozed, but McCauley wasn't sated yet. He bent the girl's left leg back up toward her crotch so she could massage her pussy with the freak foot.

"See, can you get off that way now, honey. I want to watch."

She lay back upon some pillows, features slack and stupid, and rubbed the ridge of flesh with its fused toes back and forth across her labia, making the cunt rings ping.

McCauley, who for all his fucking, hadn't come yet, sprawled across a chair and worked his meat, the friction making wet, sucky sounds. When he was just about to come, he crossed to the bed, grabbed the girl's club foot, and humped against it.

Duggan, surfing through the late-night channels, muttered "fuckin' pervert" and McCauley said, "Shut up, cocksucker," and they both laughed. Then McCauley gave a shriek, disconcertingly akin to the one he gave when leaping off a turnbuckle, and gushed all over the girl's deformed foot so it looked to Duggan like he was holding up a lump of dough covered in fresh cream.

He looked down at Carlie, who was gazing at the light fixture on the ceiling with a look that suggested an invisible metronome swinging inches above her eyes.

McCauley looked at Duggan. "She's sure stacked, but she ain't got much life in her, does she?"

Duggan popped the tab on another beer. "Ringrat," he said, and shrugged as though that explained it.

"You still got that whip you tried to whup my ass with in that match last week in Tulsa?"

"In the trunk," said Duggan, grinning.

"How 'bout let's give this little gal a spankin', see can we get some enthusiasm goin'?" He leered drunkenly, blond Prince Valiant locks sweat-slicked to his face.

Duggan got up and put his pants back on, stumbled out into the night to the car. He opened up the trunk and was leaning in when he heard something coming up fast behind. He started to turn when what felt like a bolt of red lightning exploded against the back of his skull, and he could have sworn, in his last instant of consciousness, that the dumpster itself had taken flight and slammed onto his head.

Hangover. Oh, God, what a hangover. What the hell did I drink?
That was his first thought.

Somebody coming down on top of his head with an elbow smash that went wrong, that actually connected and bounced his brain back and forth inside his skull like a pinball ricocheting between flippers—that was his second.

What the hell happened?

He heard voices lowered in conference, not the roar of the fans, and when he tried to move his arms and legs, he couldn't, and his heart lunged like it was trying to batter its way up into his throat, but his ribs caged it in where the pounding reverberated all the way up to his eyes.

"...*now*, before his friends come lookin'..."
"...no tellin' what kind of powers..."
"...gotta get some more wood..."

He caught bits of conversation, but he didn't move or open his eyes—so they'd think he was still out and, meantime, maybe he could figure out what the hell was going on.

He was outdoors—he could smell the sultry hot damp of the night and feel the gnats worrying around his ears—and he was tied with his wrists behind him around a tree or a pole of some kind. A tree, he decided, because he could feel the rough bark chafing the backs of his hands. His feet were tied, too, although he could still put his weight on them, and one ankle already felt numb, like it was going to sleep.

There were several voices.

"Shit, I think you done killed him."

"I told you his pulse is strong. You don't believe me, check it yourself."

"I believe you," said the other, followed by laughter, and another, his voice thickened with alcohol, said, "Hell, Red's not about to lay a finger on him, are you?"

"Would *you* want to?"

"Hell, I already did. I helped haul his sorry ass all the way from his car here. Son-of-a-bitch must weigh three hunnert pounds."

"Fuck, who cares if we killed him? Don't make no difference. Just keep your voices down. We ain't that far from the motel."

"You assholes." This was a new voice, flinty and slow, with an accent that sounded to Duggan like Alabama. "You can't kill the Devil with a knock on the head or even a bullet to the heart. He's faking. There's only one way to fuck up the Devil."

Oh, Jesus, thought Duggan, *this can't be for real. It can't be these loony crackers actually think that I'm—*

"Satan!" growled the last voice. "Satan only fears one thing."

That last voice was familiar. Duggan opened his eyes—and almost wished that he hadn't. He was in a wooded clearing, washed by the sickly glow of a three-quarter moon, roped to a tree. At his feet was a pile of kindling.

There were four of them, but the one Duggan's attention focused on had an Adam's apple that went up and down like an out-of-control elevator as he fidgeted with the cross at his neck. Out of uniform, Wally looked young and sickly and terrified, greasy with sweat, but in his face burned a fierce righteousness, and his eyes were like shards of black glass.

Next to him stood a scrawny, bearded man clutching a flashlight and an older man, bald as a newborn, with sharp, icy eyes and brown sticklike arms that were all tendon and bone.

Behind them a fourth one, still in his teens, took a swig from a flask every few seconds and studied Duggan with naked dread. He was tall and sloppily fat, his gut spilling over a belt buckle the size of a fist.

"Ham, look!" the fat kid said to the bearded guy. At once the flashlight was beamed into Duggan's face. He flinched back, blinded. Ham gave a drunken whoop and yelled, "It's show time, fellas. Looks like the Devil come to."

Even against four of them, Duggan knew he'd probably win in a fight, but his hands were tied so tightly he could barely feel his fingers, much less wiggle his wrists. Even if they walked away now, it would take hours to work himself free.

"Wait," he shouted, and they all looked at him with such astonishment, they might have been regarding a talking dog. "Hey, fellas, what the hell are you doing? I haven't hurt you boys."

"Shut up!" screamed Ham. He jumped up and down like a maddened monkey, then stepped forward and backhanded Duggan across the jaw with the end of the flashlight. There was a crack, and Duggan's jaw almost popped out of place. Firepoints of white agony danced in front of his eyes.

"Be still, Devil," yelled the fat teenager. Spittle shot from his pudgy lips and gleamed in the moonlight. He was clearly the youngest, with shaggy brown hair and a full, effeminate mouth, the kind of boy that, before he gained his great bulk, would have been the delight of schoolyard bullies. "We don't wanna hear your lies."

"Do it, just *do* it," hissed Wally. He held onto his cross and stared at the moon, at the ground, at the woods—anywhere but at Duggan.

"Shut up, we got time," said the Monkey. "Christ, boys, he ain't *really* be the Devil—"

Duggan felt a small spark of hope. Maybe somebody here was still borderline sane.

"He's just a *tool* of the Devil."

His hopes foundered. Were these people really that stupid— did they really believe—?

"Listen to me!" His hands might be roped behind him, his jaw aching from the blow of the flashlight, but his voice held the power to match his muscles, and it stilled them. Even Wally glanced at him, then looked away. "You men don't want to go to jail, and you will. Whatever you got in mind, you'll get caught."

"Don't listen to him," said Fat Boy. "Light the wood! Light it! Burn his ass for what he did to McCauley!"

It took all Duggan's nerve to control his voice, to speak as if he were trying to talk the promoter into a bigger cut of pay, not negotiating for his life.

"You boys are just trying to scare the shit out of me, right? And doing a helluva job, let me tell you. You all know wrestling's a fake. McCauley wasn't hurt tonight. If you go back to the motel, you'll find him in Room 15. Him and Hacksaw Ames along with some prime pussy. Might share it with you if you ask 'em nice."

"Liar! We saw you blind McCauley! We saw the fireball!"

"It's a trick, a simple trick you boys could do yourselves. A puff of smoke, some sparks. McCauley's not blind. Hell, McCauley and I go bass fishing when we're off work, we're good friends." They were staring at him, not answering, so he pressed on, embellishing with a few lies. "Our kids play together. I wouldn't hurt McCauley's ass—our feud is bringing in big bucks all over the country."

The blond kid, face flushed as though the mere thought of such heresy was a personal betrayal, spat back, "We saw the blood. What about the blood?"

"And don't tell us it's no chicken blood either," yelled the bald one.

"No, boys, I'm not gonna lie to you. The blood's real, all right. But McCauley cut his head open himself."

They gaped at him. He had their interest now. Maybe…

"One of McCauley's fingers was taped, remember? Well, there's a blade hidden inside the tape. Wrestlers do it all the time. Guy falls out of the ring, rubs his head where he hit it—you can't see nothing—he's cutting his forehead. It's not deep, but it bleeds like a bitch."

There was a beat of quiet. Duggan listened for the sound of a car. He wondered why Hacksaw and McCauley hadn't started to search for him by now. But then Hacksaw was probably still sound asleep and McCauley'd let his mother be kidnapped by terrorists before he'd pull out of a piece of gash.

"Evil liar." It was Wally talking. "He's Satan come in human form. It's evil moves his tongue. I *saw* him burn McCauley. Now burn *him*."

"We will burn him," said Ham. "But first let's see the color of his blood." He clicked open a switchblade. Almost before Duggan had time to register the pain, the tip gashed him from nipple to navel, tracing the lines of the "X" in his chest hair. Blood poured down Duggan's belly, pooling over his belt, streaming down his jeans and into his boots.

Terror prodded Duggan to greater rage. He wanted to scream for help, to bellow out to the great dark night for someone, anyone, to help him, but he wasn't quite to that point yet, couldn't allow it, so instead he shouted, "You fucking yokels! It's a business, an act. Like the movies, for Christ's sake. I'm just a guy trying to earn a living."

"Shut up," said Fat Boy, grabbing a branch from the pile at Duggan's feet. He struck a match, lit it.

The flames licked across the boy's sweaty, acned face in lurid stripes.

Duggan felt his will cave in. He ached with fear. In his life-time, he'd imagined a dozen ways to die—a neck-breaking fall from a turnbuckle or a crash in the Cessna he flew for recreation, but not this—not the passive, helpless death of a trussed and burning captive.

Fat Boy was tormenting him with the flame, touching it almost to the kindling, drawing it back at the last instant before it caught. The others hooted, egging him on.

Fat Boy touched the red tip of the flame to Duggan's bleeding chest.

"Jesus, don't do this," pleaded Duggan. "I've got a family, a wife. I've got kids at home. I'm no devil. Don't do this."

"He's lying!" screamed Wally, and his mica eyes blazed.

Pete Duggan was not a praying man, but in his youth he'd spent a few Sundays at the First Baptist church in Fresno, and his second wife was a Born Again Christian. Now he felt the start of a desperate, terrified prayer form on his lips.

Not this, God, he thought, *not like this,* and there was a moment of awful, horrific clarity when all the things he might have been, had ever dreamed of being, crystallized in his soul, and it seemed unbelievable and bitter and mean that his adult life had been squandered in an endless round of tacky arenas and auditoriums smelling of beer and puke and promoters' farts, getting spit on and cussed at and hated and, *oh Jesus, not burning, anything except this...*

He heard sirens.

Not just one siren, but many.

Headlights knifed through the trees, then disappeared. More headlights, headed up the road behind the Greenway.

"I'll go check," said Fat Boy and started to run.

Duggan saw the red flasher atop a police car strobe past the line of trees. He thought about yelling out, but knew no one would hear him. The sirens were a wildly keening song now, the screaming of madwomen.

Minutes later, Fat Boy slid down the embankment. "It's the motel," he panted. "The Greenway Motel's on fire. Come on, we gotta get outta here. There's police cars and fire engines everywhere. We so much as light a cigarette, they'll see us."

The lit branch was extinguished as the men scattered into the dark.

Leaving Duggan alone. Alive.

The sirens sounded like the caroling of evil angels. A shadow separated itself from the trees. He almost started to scream before he realized it was Carlie. Her blouse was ripped and badly buttoned, her face so pallid he imagined he could see the outline of the bony mask underneath. She was barefoot and the lower half of her deformed foot was black with soot, making it almost hooflike.

"I thought they were gonna burn you. Those fucking fools."

"Untie me," said Duggan, straining against his bonds.

She stared at him, waxen-eyed. Duggan thought she must have fled the fire and might be in shock. "It's okay now. They've gone. Just help me get loose."

She stared in the direction that the men had run. "Those wretched, blundering swine—"

"Untie me. I'll go teach them bastards a lesson."

"Cowardly piss drinkers. Eaters of offal." She cocked her head at Duggan, smiled. "Not because of what they did, but what they *didn't* do."

As she spoke, the color returned to her face, and her dead eyes lit up, full of vigor and spite. She walked toward Duggan and, with a swift move of one hand, unzipped him and released his penis, bestowed upon its lolling end a savage kiss of teeth.

Duggan howled.

She licked blood from her lips.

"Your friends didn't make it out of the fire. They burned to death."

"Then how did you get out if they..."

"Your angle is that you're a Servant of Satan, but you're just another arrogant fool. Disrespectful. Blasphemous. And Satan will not be mocked."

In her face blazed a feral joy that iced Duggan's bones.

She walked away from him, fully twenty paces before turning back. With measure and grace, she stretched out one languid hand toward him and made a gesture with her wrist, both beautiful and beckoning. Her fingertips began to glow. The glow spread up her arm. A ball of flame the size of a soccer ball roared the length of her arm, out her finger and onto the wood collected at Duggan's feet.

It torched.

Duggan's screams rent the night.

Carlie smiled and whiffed the smoke that curled from her fingertips.

"You idiot," she muttered, looking back in the direction of the flaming motel. "You wouldn't know the Devil if She were standing right beside you."

Idol

Conners felt his dick stiffen as the bronze god with flowing blond hair and a six-foot python draped around his shoulders made his way toward the wrestling ring. Raw desire, one part longing to two parts lust, thrilled through him like a hit of speed. No matter how many times he saw Darius the Python wrestle, he was always awed by the man—those slablike pecs oiled to a sheen, sculpted deltoids and laddered abs, a butt so perfectly tight and square it made Conners' balls ache to look at it.

If only...

If only I could make love with the most perfect man alive. If only I could be his slave. Belong to him. Become so close that we were one.

Conners thought of the scrap of paper in his jeans, the one with the dates and the cities. Friday, July 15, the Coliseum in Richmond, Virginia; Saturday, July 16, the Civic Center in Roanoke, Virginia; Sunday, Dorton Arena in Raleigh, North Carolina.... Today was Tuesday at the Coliseum in Greenville, South Carolina. Three days to get to Richmond in time to see the Python's next performance.

Unlike Darius, who flew first-class from match to match, Conners drove a decrepit Mustang, which he fueled with gas by working odd jobs as he went along: cleaning up trash in the arenas, selling programs and wrestling souvenirs.

Shit work, sure, but he had to earn a living.

While he waited and lusted and longed.

Dreaming about his "if onlys"....

"You're crazy," his ex-lover Ric had told him on the phone a month before when Conners, in a weak moment, had made the mistake of calling him. "You're fucking obsessed. You've thrown away your life and somebody who really loves you for a man you don't even know, one who won't look at you twice once he's had a piece of your ass."

Conners had tried to explain that it didn't matter, that if he was with Darius only one time, it would be worth all the sacrifices. But then he'd made a big mistake. He'd confessed to Ric how it was like that song he used to listen to, an old Carly Simon number called "Stardust" and how, in it, Carly sings about an unrequited love for a movie star whose "stardust is golden," and how she's sure that just one touch and she'll be golden, too, as golden as her lover, and...

Ric's derisive laughter had been the last thing Conners heard before slamming down the phone.

So he'd lost Ric. What the fuck, there were a thousand Rics in the world, a million like him. There was only one Darius. Darius had reached the ring by now and was handing down his living namesake to his flunky manager, an ex-wrestler named McCoy who waited outside the ring. Darius raised his huge arms and strutted and flexed. He lifted the amulet he wore around his neck, a small obsidian python, and kissed its ruby eyes. The crowd jeered and hurled paper cups.

Jealous, thought Conners. Men and women both. Darius was a consummate heel (as the bad guys were called in pro-wrestling lingo), but also a number-one draw, the World Wrestling League's biggest attraction, a legend, in fact, who'd been wrestling under one name or another for over two decades. His spectacular physique and seemingly perpetual youth prompted the envious and inferior to concoct dark tales, weird rumors—that Darius was evil, inhuman, possessed, that the live python who always accompanied Darius to the ring was more than just a prop or pet but a demon in command of Darius's soul.

Just bullshit wrestling hype, thought Conners, cooked up by bumpkin fans.

Fans like that ditzy punk kid in Akron. Conners still remembered the kid, even though the encounter had been almost four months ago, when Conners had just left school and home and lover to follow Darius, to follow his dream of "if only."

The kid had popped up backstage at the Akron Coliseum where Conners had been waiting, hoping for a glimpse of Darius. He was pale and pimply and anorexically thin, dressed in grungy black jeans and a sweat-stained black T-shirt with Darius's picture on the front—albino mane and blindingly cobalt eyes— the same picture that adorned the tight blue body shirt that Conners was wearing now.

"Ringrat?" the kid had said, looking him up and down.

Conners was so green to the game he didn't even know what the word meant.

"Ringrat?" repeated the kid. His breath had a sour metallic tang, the hardcore reek of semen and piss. Conners had taken a step backward.

"Ringrat," the kid said knowingly, a statement this time. "I seen you at a half dozen coliseums in two weeks. You want to turn a trick? The Mad Turk and the Mongol are bored waiting to go on. They sent me out to find them a pretty face to fuck."

Up to that point, Conners had done his share of tricking in his twenty years, but this was different. He shook his head, partly "no" and partly in amazement at what he was about to say.

"I'm not here for the Turk or the Mongol or anybody else," he said with unexpected pride. "I'm here for Darius. When he wants me. If he wants me. Just Darius."

Although it didn't seem possible, the kid turned two shades paler than he already was, as if his very blood was being vamp-irized before Conners's eyes. "You stupid fuck," he muttered, backing away with such palpable fear that Conners almost expect-ed him to make the sign of the cross. "Asshole, don't you know it's the pretty ones like you the Python wants?"

It was meant as a warning obviously, but Conners took it as a promise, as encouragement. *The pretty ones.* Well, it was hard taking care of yourself on the road, but Conners had managed to keep his looks. He was small and boyishly slight, but well-toned and sleekly muscled, and he kept his body almost as deeply tanned as the Python's with daily sunbathing sessions stretched out across the hood of his car.

By now, he'd heard the rumors, too, about just how partic-ular the Python was. He didn't choose his lovers casually or often and sometimes "auditioned" for the right one from a group of three or four. In the age of safe sex, Conners figured Darius was probably just being careful, opting for quality over quantity, the classy trick over the easy score.

It's the pretty ones like you the Python wants.

He'd cherished that phrase, held it in his mind like a mantra, a source of comfort and hope. And meanwhile his obsession deepened. His lust for Darius eclipsed desire for all other men, and his life pre-Darius—lovers and studies and job—took on the grainy quality of a dream he'd only just awoken from the first time he laid eyes on the golden wrestler.

Stardust, your stardust is golden....

Maybe it had something to do with being small physically or with coming from a dirt-poor Indiana farm family where his dad always treated him with thinly veiled contempt—the runt of the litter, younger brother to two muscular brute brothers—but Conners had always felt wretchedly inadequate, that he could never be good enough. As a youth, vague longings and dis-satisfactions had wheeled and circled in his head like carrion-eating birds and when he lay awake, late in the night, listening to Carly Simon crooning on the Walkman and fighting insomnia by beating his meat instead of counting sheep, it was a phantom lover to whom he cried out as he came, a man so powerful, so beautiful that all Conners's weaknesses would be obliterated by that lover's radiance, and he would be consumed.

Years later, at a wrestling match that he'd attended with some friends, he had first seen Darius in all his glorious flesh, the lover of his dreams, his heart's obsession.

Darius, whose magic would rub off on him, who would make him golden, too.

Darius, who, at this very moment, was smashing Hangman Hughes with a flying dropkick that sent the Hangman somersaulting over the top rope and sprawling onto the concrete. Every time the Hangman would try to climb back into the ring, Darius would boot him back out. Finally Darius leaped out of the ring and knocked Ivan upside down onto the concrete and into presumed insensibility.

Pandemonium ensued.

The fans hurled epithets and paper cups and beer cans.

The bell rang and the gnomelike ref scurried around the ring waving his stumpy arms, calling for a disqualification.

In the midst of this, Conners suddenly looked over and caught McCoy, who was stationed at ringside, ogling his crotch as if it was an eclair on a dessert tray. The man's tiny, scat-colored eyes were like drillbits hammered into his skull. McCoy edged over and leaned down. Spraying spittle into Conners's ear, he hissed, "Tonight's your lucky night, son. Come back after everyone leaves. Darius wants to try you out."

Late at night, with the matches over and the crowd gone home, the quiet of the Coliseum made footfalls in the empty corridors sound to Conners like sharply struck anvil blows. As promised, a basement door had been left ajar. McCoy, eyes beady as a lurking troll's, was waiting for him inside.

"This way," he said and guided Conners down a corridor with doors that opened into a series of dressing rooms. They descended a stairway that smelled of beer and popcorn into a sub-basement area, then continued along another corridor to a locker room, where McCoy told him to strip and shower.

"You won't need them clothes," McCoy growled when Conners reached for his jeans afterward. "The Python wants you naked."

Conners's blood was thundering, much of it going directly to his cock, which stood already erect, the pink crown bobbing against his flat belly.

"Now don't get disappointed if you ain't the one chose," said McCoy, leering down at Conners's hard-on. "The Python's real particular. He don't have a boy but once a month or so."

The revelation that he wouldn't be the only one made Conners's throat constrict with disappointment, but there was no time to respond. McCoy produced a key and unlocked a metal door. Inside was darkness. As Conners hesitated, McCoy's hand drove into the small of his back, shoving him forward. Before Conners's eyes adjusted to the dim light, the smell assailed him: sweat and urine and the musky tang of cum. And noises: the smack and grunt and panting of rutting males.

Then he turned a corner around a set of lockers and rocked back on his heels. There was a wrestling ring set up and, in it, four slender, naked young men. And in the center of the ring, resplendently, goldenly naked, Darius sprawled splay-legged in a leather sling that had been attached to some overhead cables. His mouth was open and his long hair hung down as the boys took turns directing streams of piss on him. Piss drops gleamed on his skin, glittered in his pale hair like a shower of sapphires.

"Go on, get in the ring," said McCoy, coming up behind Conners. "And don't forget, whatever happens here tonight, you ain't seen nothin'. Darius paid the nightwatchmen off real good to let him use this place after hours."

Trembling with anticipation, Conners climbed into the ring just as a dark-haired boy with a thick, bulb-headed cock seized the sling and shoved Darius backward. Ass in the air, he swung on collision course with the erect dick of the amply endowed boy behind him. Conners heard a wet thwack and saw the slicked meat disappear between taut, muscular buttocks. Impaled to the hilt, Darius groaned. Then the swing reversed its direction. The cock pulled free with a wet, popping sound. Darius hung his head back while the sequence was repeated, his pale, piss-soaked hair hanging down in lank strands so that, to Conners, he resembled a degraded Zeus.

Darius raised his head and appraised those servicing him.

In this light, the fierce blue eyes gleamed pale silver, as though icicles had been plunged through his eye sockets.

His coldly seductive stare came to rest on Conners. "You, the last addition to the harem," he said. "You look good and clean and healthy. Show me what you can do."

Conners was more than ready to perform. The only thing that mildly flummoxed him was seeing Darius in the sling. From everything he'd ever heard, Darius's rep was as a consummate topman. To see the world famous grappler with his ass in the air, ready for reaming, startled Conners so badly he almost lost some of his erection.

That didn't last, though. As he approached the sling, Darius's voice filled the room, a rich commanding baritone. "You'll start by sucking my dick and eating out my ass. Then you can lick the piss off me."

Conners positioned himself between Darius's elevated legs. Darius's cock was uncut and thickly veined, leading to a pair of heavy balls lightly furred with gold hair. Conners sucked the hefty stob into his mouth, relishing the salty tang of pre-cum on the crown.

He moved down, slurping juice across the heavy balls, then parted the perfect rectangular slabs of Darius's cheeks with his hands. The wrestler's asshole was a perfect purple rose, puckered and wet from earlier explorations by his other suitors.

Conners widened it with two fingers, probed it with his tongue. Hunger, at once terrible and thrilling, welled up and overflowed him. He wanted to eat his way into Darius's ass, up into his belly all the way to his red pumping heart. He wanted to gorge himself on the sweet treasures of Darius's belly and chest, to burrow in and become one with his idol.

It was as if the force of his lust gave off a scent that was palpable even in a room that already reeked of sex.

Darius lifted up his head and focused those cut-glass eyes on Conners, saying, "You others—leave. This one…stays…with me."

The other boys sulked and glared, but, with McCoy herding them, moodily complied.

When they were alone, Darius fingered the stone python at his neck and said, "I noticed you staring at my little idol here. Do you know what it represents?"

"The Python," said Conners, feeling stupid. "Your name."

Darius rocked himself gently in the sling. He seemed amused. "I got this many years ago from a man who made his fortune wrestling pythons in North Africa. He was a very beautiful man, very wise. He worshipped Satan in the form of a python. Do you know what happened to him?"

Conners shook his head.

"I killed him when I took this idol from him."

There was a beat of silence before Darius said, "Does that matter to you? That I killed someone?"

Conners stared into those dazzling, incandescent eyes and knew, from the bottom of his heart, that it did not. His desire was beyond good and bad, beyond self-preservation.

"No," he heard himself say. "No, it doesn't."

"And do you believe the rumors—that I've sold myself to Satan?" asked Darius, suppressed mirth curling the corners of his mouth.

"No."

"Would it matter to you if I had?"

Without hesitation: "No."

"Good. Your lack of scruples makes you all the more desirable. Now let's see what you can do. I'm empty. See if you can fill me."

Conners grabbed the sides of the sling and pulled Darius toward him. His cock penetrated the tight circle of muscle and entered the plush, dark warmth of Darius's interior. The inner muscles played Conners's penis like a lute. Moaning, he drove into Darius with all his weight, wishing his dick were long enough to penetrate past Darius's heart and pop out of his mouth like an enormous tongue.

"Stop!" ordered Darius.

Conners did so.

"Pull out."

He complied.

"How big is that cock of yours? Let me see it."

Conners moved around so Darius could see his seven rigid inches.

Darius's silvery eyeballs peered from under slitted lids.

"It isn't big enough. Use your fist. Use your whole arm. Fill me."

The flesh underneath Darius's ribcage was deflating, expanding, deflating again. As if his whole body were gripped with the contractions of his enormous appetite.

Conners spit on his fingers and inserted two, then three, four, into Darius's ass.

"More!"

His entire hand was engulfed now. Slowly Conners curled the fingers into a fist and began to thrust. The sling swayed and Darius's body shook from the pounding.

"It's not enough. I...need...more."

Conners pushed his wrist and forearm inside. He fucked until his biceps ached, ramming his whole arm in elbow-deep.

Darius began to shake and moan, as though his very skeletal system were unhinging.

Somewhere in Conners's mind, it occurred to him that he must be hurting the man, that he could be doing serious internal damage and that he should withdraw, but the realization only drove him to greater brutality. He loved Darius, but he wanted to hurt him, too; the hurting was part of the having. Faster and faster, his arm pistoned, fist-fucking his idol like a boxer battering a helpless, ropebound opponent.

"More!"

The wrestler's ribcage heaved like staves about to burst. The flesh of his abdomen went concave, convex, concave again, as though a bellows were working in his guts.

"More!"

Conners felt it then, the first mighty contraction inside Darius's rectum. It felt like his fist was snagged in undertow, like he was elbow-deep in quicksand.

Darius's sphincter muscle suddenly tightened on Conners's arm just underneath the elbow. Conners was getting ready to pull back for another ramming. He couldn't free his arm. His flesh was clamped as if in the maw of a shark.

Conners couldn't believe what was happening. Leaning back, he twisted to try to extricate his arm.

Nothing happened, or rather something did...something began to happen, but Conners was so stunned at first that it took a moment for him to recover his breath sufficiently to scream.

His arm was being drawn in. Inexorably, efficiently, in rhythmic powerful waves. Like a bandsaw pulling a cord of wood into the feeder.

"What is this? What's happening?"

"MORE!"

Conners's arm continued to disappear. Past the forearm, around the angle of the elbow. Darius's gut began to bloat beneath the pressure of the flesh it was stretching to accommodate.

"No!" screamed Conners. He was bicep-deep now in Darius's bowels, his arm throbbing as though constricted inside a giant blood-pressure cuff. He shrieked as bones began to give way, fingers and wrist bones being pulverized, his elbow shattering.

In a frenzy powered by agony, he fought to retract his arm, but Darius' asshole tightened and contracted with merciless force. His shoulder dislocated loudly. It stretched away from his body at an impossible angle and was swallowed up.

Conners felt the world tilting under him in neon waves.

He tried to stay on his feet, because to fall meant adding pressure to his dislocated arm, but he was growing giddy with pain.

"No, please! Don't do this!"

Darius looked up through eyes sheened as if with ice. "Oh, I must. In order to stay young and beautiful. Like my predecessor, who worshipped pythons, I have to take my nourishment this way. After all, I am part python."

He gave a hellish grimace, like a woman in the last throes of a fatal labor. The hole between his buttocks distended wider, became a well impossibly deep and wide.

With a final scream Conners sank to his knees. Darius gave another huge contraction and sucked the rubbery meat of

Conners's shoulder in up to his neck. Bones and tendons, ligaments were being crushed, reduced. Conners's head was forced to one side at an impossible angle. Vertebrae unhinged. His bulging eyes wept blood. With the final snap of his spine, he became a quadriplegic.

And Darius opened himself up even wider until he could draw in Conners's lolling head.

Conners was still conscious as his face moved like a pallid slug into that moist and fetid dark. By now, he was long past terror, and sanity was a remnant from another lifetime. The pain was gone, his ruined synapses incapable of transmission.

A strange and languid peace, black and tropically warm as the bizarre new world he was entering, enveloped him. He was becoming one with Darius. Soon his flesh and bone and marrow would be part of his; he would go into the ring with Darius, would eat and shit and fuck with Darius, would live and die with Darius. They would be forever one.

It was like being born again, into the awful core of a dark and reeking universe and yet, as Conners's skull was slowly crushed, his dying brain put on a pyrotechnic dazzle brilliant enough to offset the other horrors. Gaudy lightning strobed behind his eyes.

It was as if he were showered in stardust.

Knockouts

It was the sea that brought him the first one.

Charlie had been awake most of the night, tossing and turning and beating his meat in his one uncooled room. Finally he could stand his state of sweaty arousal no longer. Pulling on a pair of shorts and a tropical shirt, he went outside. The beach was on the other side of A1-A, a few hundred yards via a plank walkway through tall marsh grass. He could hear the muted suck and thunder of the waves as he approached it.

The night was sultry, moist, heavy with heat and the soft, throbbing whir of insects. He stepped off the planking onto powdery brown sand just as the first tendrils of pink touched the horizon like a faint lipstick smear.

He was looking at that pink smear or he wouldn't have seen her, the lone swimmer, her flailing arm a dark bar briefly bisecting the light. He took a few steps toward the sea. By that time he could hear her screams.

Charlie stripped his shirt off, took a few running steps through the surf, and hurled himself into the ocean.

The next few minutes were still a black blur to him. He wasn't that strong a swimmer, having grown up in rural Indiana and moved to Florida only the year before, scrounging for manual labor jobs in the wake of Hurricane Andrew. The tide was high, the sea hungry, eager for the chance to drink down two victims instead of one.

Cold and frightened, already swallowing brine, Charlie wanted to turn back. But a part of his mind, the stern, angry, whip-wielding part, wouldn't allow him to falter. A woman was in danger. Charlie's mother had brought him up to think of women as special, sacred, superior in every way to men, who were filthy-minded and wanted only one thing. Women were to be placed upon a pedestal, protected, cherished. A real man would risk his life for one in danger.

So Charlie floundered on.

He had lost sight of her, was treading water in the trough of a wave, when suddenly she skidded down the side of an oncoming wall of water like a bodysurfer out of control. She crashed into Charlie and wrapped her arms around him in a death grip. She was a small woman, but panic made her fiercely strong. She was climbing up onto Charlie's shoulders, forcing him underwater.

Charlie struggled to keep his head above the surface. A wave lifted and flung them. Charlie looked into the woman's terror-stricken eyes and felt his dick get stiff. He made a fist and drove it hard into the woman's jaw. Her eyes rolled back.

He swung an arm around her neck and started breaststroking toward shore.

The beach was still deserted when Charlie reached it. He picked the woman up, chuckling to himself as he got a mental image of King Kong lifting Fay Wray, carried her up the bank into the tall marsh grass and laid her on the ground.

In the dark, Charlie couldn't see her well. He liked that. It meant she didn't have a face, not really, she didn't even exist. She was a secret between him and the ocean.

He stepped out of his shorts.

Always respect a woman, his mother used to say.

He yanked the woman's sopping tank suit down over her ankles.

Put her on a pedestal. Treat her like a queen.

He rammed his dick inside her, sand, sea water, and all. It hurt but Charlie was too excited to care. He fucked and fucked, and he wanted so bad to come, he was dying to come, but he couldn't, he…just…couldn't…, and about that time the woman moaned and started to come around, so he slugged her again, and she sagged back onto the sand with a little trickle of blood coming out of her mouth.

Put a woman on a pedestal, treat her like gold, keep those nasty-boy ideas out of your head.

He thrust in sweaty, grunting desperation, like a man trying to dig a grave with his cock, but he still couldn't come—he could *never* come—and it made him furious, so he waited until the woman started to come to and then he punched her again…and again and again…until he came with a roar that he muffled by biting into the flesh of her tit, but there was no pleasure in it, he felt like his balls were being pulled out of the hole in his cock, and his cheeks were soaked with tears of rage and disgust that he had let his mother down.

But he was done. Finally.

For now.

Sore and exhausted, Charlie retrieved his clothes. The sun had just risen over the edge of the horizon like a buttered bun in a pop-up toaster. He squinted down at the woman. There wasn't a lot of her face left, but she was still breathing. Charlie walked down to the edge of the ocean and washed the blood off his knuckles.

He went home and dressed for work and spent the day pushing wheelbarrows full of cement around the construction site of a motel that was being rebuilt after being flattened by Andrew. His dick didn't give him much trouble, even when a couple of schoolgirls flounced by, giggling and giving the workmen the eye, and he didn't think of the drowned woman again until the next day when the *Miami Herald* carried a headline about the brutal rape-murder of a Wyoming tourist named Deborah Engels visiting Miami for a nursing convention.

That one, the first one, was for free. That was the one the sea gave him.

After that, Charlie kept trying to achieve satisfaction the way he usually did. Alone, in the privacy of his torrid little room, he would beat his seven inches till the crown purpled and bled, and he thought about Deborah Engels and about the pleasure that had shot hand-to-groin when his fist slammed into her face, but he still didn't come. He bought overpriced magazines wrapped in cellophane with names like *Buxom Bondagettes* and *Babes in Torment* and fantasized about what he'd like to do to them, but his dick remained recalcitrant, like a gun you could cock but not fire. (Because women belonged on pedestals, after all, Mama had said, and no nasty man should even want to put his hands on them—let alone shoot jism all over their pictures.)

On those infrequent occasions when she'd caught him masturbating as a boy, Mama had used a leather riding crop to reenforce the notion that God intended dicks for peeing only and male minds should be kept as white and clean as a freshly scrubbed-out, never-shat-in toilet.

Yet even now, despite the bad memories, Charlie kept a photo of his mother on the table by the bed: hatted for church, sultry as a Florida August in her faux pearls and heavy make-up. Looking like a whore and acting like a saint as she wagged her cutie-pie ass up to the rail to take Communion from a minister who peeked down her cleavage as he slid the wafer onto her tongue.

Sometimes, in desperation, Charlie turned his mother's picture to the wall, although he felt guilty doing so; at other times he stared at it as though hypnotized. Next to the photo, he kept another fetish object, an agate statuette of a buxum, naked woman on an inch-high pedestal. Charlie had won the paper-weight throwing balls through wooden hoops at a carnival back in Indiana when he was only twelve. For years it had stayed hidden at the back of his closet. Now, far from Mama's prying eyes, he could admire this trophy salvaged from a wretched adolescence during which whippings with the riding crop were as much a part of the weekly routine as the trek to church. Charlie liked to look at the woman's mottled agate breasts, her stone cooze shot through with vermillion, and remember his mother's favorite saying about how women should be put on pedestals. Charlie thought that this was the only kind of pedestal women belonged on, posing nude for a man's pleasure like some kind of circus animal. It made him feel more powerful to think such thoughts, more in control, but, lately, it didn't help him climax.

Before he pulled the woman from the sea, Charlie had been able to come, if not regularly or reliably, then at least often enough so as not to feel half-crazy with frustration. But after the morning on the beach with Deborah Engels, it was as if his mother's voice in Charlie's head got nastier, meaner. It interrupted his lushest fantasies with cries of *Pervert! Degenerate!* It stopped him on the verge of shooting off a wad so many times he finally wept with longing and wanted to bang his head into the wall until he slumped unconscious. It was as if his mother were there in the room with him, as if she leaned over his humid bed and shrieked while he rubbed himself raw.

He was growing desperate, thinking about ways to hurt himself, wondering if pain might be enough to make him come, when he made the decision not to wait for another gift from the sea, but to take the next one himself.

Her name was Peggy Ingersoll. In her late twenties, she was already spent-looking. Nicotine had scraped all melodiousness from her voice; alcohol had left her jowly and bloated, with a case of the shakes if you encountered her before her first shot of the morning.

Charlie would sit next to her at the Seabreeze Bar after work, downing rail drinks and occasionally, when he was feeling flush, buying a few for Peggy. That was enough to cinch their friendship; the mere scent of gin made her purr like a stroked alleycat. For a fifth slipped into her purse, she'd meet Charlie out back of the Seabreeze and take his cock in her red-lipsticked mouth or into the cleft of her tattooed tits. Though her sucking was lusty, almost frantic, as if she were performing mouth-to-dick resuscitation, Charlie would get just to the point of climax and then bog down. He just couldn't let go.

And Peggy always looked defeated, like his failure to spurt was somehow a black mark on what must otherwise have been a pristine cocksucking record.

"It ain't your fault, babe," Charlie told her. "I prob'ly had a mite too much to drink is all."

Peggy shrugged, still doing her imitation of a Hoover. "Usually too much booze just makes 'em limp. You're hard as a cop's nightstick, honey."

He didn't want to hit Peggy. He really didn't. She looked as if life had roughed her up enough, with sixty years of hard times in her thirty-year-old alkie eyes and a booze gut that made her look like she had a bun halfway to done in her oven.

He didn't want to hurt her, but then he saw her one night, heading from her daytime job at a Hialeah Hojo's up A1-A toward the Seabreeze. By that time, Charlie was going into his fiftieth hour of arousal-induced sleep deprivation, and his cock was abraded from his desperate efforts to get release.

Charlie was driving his '81 Chrysler, headed for the Seabreeze himself. He swung up to the curb. Peggy got in without a word, as if she'd been expecting him to drive by and pick her up. Her expression, dull-eyed, defeated, told Charlie all he needed to know: she was already brutalized by life, he could hardly do worse by her.

He didn't take her to the Seabreeze, of course, but along a dirt road heading toward the beach, after stopping for a six-pack at a convenience store. The dark enfolded them like protective wings. Love bugs, locked in airborne copulation, buzzed in buggy lewdness around their heads.

Charlie suggested a stroll up the beach. Peggy was on her third Bud already. She grabbed a fourth for the road, and they meandered up the dark beach, the sea seething at their ankles, beer rumbling in their guts.

When they stopped next to a darkened dune, Peggy drained the last of the beer and dropped with a grunt to her knees, fumbling for Charlie's zipper. He let her take him out and into her mouth, all sloppy with beery saliva.

When he was thoroughly lubricated, Charlie lifted her to her feet.

"Let's do somethin' different tonight, honey."

He'd figured a straight fuck ought to be no problem. But she surprised him by flat out refusing.

"I don't do that," she said. "I do hand and I do mouth, but no pussy. I don't do pussy."

"Why not?"

"Are you crazy? I don't want to get AIDS."

"I got rubbers."

"They break."

But he'd made up his mind. He had to come. If he waited one minute longer, his brains were going to explode out the end of his dick like so much white cheese.

"I'm sorry, honey," he said and swung a mean right into Peggy's jaw. She went down, but there was still fight in her. She rolled to the side and tried to scurry away. Charlie grabbed a fistful of hair and twisted her around, popped her in the chin till she folded, then threw her back, kicked her legs apart, and released his dick, which bounced forth like a cage-crazy hound while he tore off her panties and mounted her.

For long minutes he lay there, thrusting himself into her unresistant form, bruising the head of his dick and bruising her face, and every time he hit her, his dick would strain and stiffen until it felt like the blood vessels along the shaft were going to pop like overstretched hemorrhoids, but the voice was ranting in his head, as Mama of the Whip intoned, *You put a woman on a pedestal, respect her. You never, ever hit a woman,* and everytime the voice said that, Charlie battered Peggy's face, but he didn't come and after twenty or so minutes, his erection died away of sheer exhaustion, and Peggy just plain died.

The experience with Peggy was so unsatisfactory that for a few weeks Charlie didn't even try to jerk off. He stopped buying *Buxum Bondagettes* and the rest of the SM rags and got reeling drunk every night, so smashed that his cock couldn't have gotten up even if ten naked babes in bondage had squirmed hogtied across the floor of his bedroom.

Then one night some of the guys on the construction job were going to a place called Pure Platinum, a pussy palace near Coconut Grove, famed for a bevy of blondes whom the wonders of diet and cosmetic surgery had endowed with wasp waists and Barbie-doll boobs and the wheat hair of lushly maned ponies. Pure Platinum was known for some mildly kinky extras, like naked trapeze acts and jello wrestling contests. Tonight, when Charlie and his buddies drove up, the sign on the marquee read: KNOCK-OUTS: ALL GIRL BOXING, 10 P.M.

"Hey, what the fuck," Charlie said, "do they actually hit each other?"

"Naw, it's all fake," said Cleeg, a scrawny dude from west Texas with a goiter the size of a golf ball twanging in his neck. "They just poof around at each other with them little gloves. Don't wanna mess up them pretty faces or put a dent in them silicone tits."

Put a woman on a pedestal, treat her like a queen.

Charlie's dick, although already tranquilized with half a dozen bourbons, began to stir.

"C'mon," said Cleeg, "let's watch them bitches fight."

As it turned out, Cleeg was right about the quality of the boxing. The fights were stagey and silly, more like sorority girls boffing each other with pillows than anything approximating real boxing. Their one redeeming value was that the girls performed topless, melonous mammaries bouncing in sweet parody of their gloved hands. Toward the end, though, there was a girl named Roxane, tall and long-limbed with a thoroughbred ass and the kind of sleekly packed biceps that suggested significant time spent in weight rooms; she boxed with an energy that went beyond show, delivering a few well-placed, if pulled punches, that left her opponent's face splotchy red.

"Wow," Cleeg said, "what a knock-out she is," and for a second Charlie gaped at him, thinking Cleeg had said something outrageously filthy, even for Cleeg. Then he realized Cleeg just meant the girl was pretty.

"Yeah, I wouldn't mind getting into those boxing trunks."

"In your dreams," said Cleeg, "in your dreams."

In his dreams. She walked into an uppercut that imbedded her lower teeth in the roof of her mouth like stalactites while her legs, like the gates to Paradise, swung wide before him, and he poured himself into her, coming and coming while the unspilled seed of a thousand fruitless masturbatory sessions gushed from his dick in milky torrents, and he woke up moaning, rutting wildly into the mattress, but the voice in his head screamed *Nasty! Filthy!* and the hole in the head of his penis might as well have been plugged with cement.

He woke up with his face twisted toward the nightstand, where Mama of the Whip and the Naked Lady on the Pedestal eyed his pitiful efforts at self-pleasuring with cold disdain.

Never hit a woman. Put her on a pedestal. Treat her like a queen.

Charlie hadn't come since the morning on the beach with Deborah Engels almost two months earlier. Peggy had been a disaster, but maybe that was because the booze had already done a number on her face and body even before Charlie's fists got into the act. Charlie decided he needed someone sexier. He needed Roxane, topless and slick with sweat in her red satin boxing trunks.

So he began to plan it.

At first he thought of grabbing Roxane when she left Pure Platinum, but that was no good, because a bouncer walked the girls to their cars. Nobody came to meet the girls when they arrived, however, and Charlie soon learned that Roxane didn't get to work until 9:30 P.M.

When she arrived at the club a few nights later, Charlie was parked nearby. Roxane got out of her Datsun wearing jeans and a black sweatshirt with the logo of a local gym on the front, carrying a tote bag that must have contained her costume. Charlie ambled over and asked if she'd autograph a picture he'd taken of her for a buddy. She looked Charlie over like he was week-old bread and said she was in a hurry. Charlie showed her a twenty, which she palmed with greed almost as naked as her body had been in the skimpy boxing trunks.

"Here, let me get the picture," said Charlie, lifting the trunk of his car. As it opened, Roxane took a step backward.

Charlie yanked her forward by the hair. Before she could scream, he punched her in the side of the head—one, two—fast and hard, threw her sideways into the trunk, tossed her tote bag in on top of her, roped her hands behind her and slammed the trunk shut.

He got behind the wheel. In all, the subduing and abduction of Roxane had taken less than twenty seconds.

Charlie drove back to his efficiency on A1-A, careful to stay just below the speed limit and come to a full stop at all red lights. At home, he parked so the trunk was only a few feet from the front door, slung Roxane over his shoulder, and carried her inside—an exposure time he figured was less than ten seconds and was virtually invisible in the ill-lit rental complex.

Inside he threw Roxane across the bed, stripped off her jeans and underpants and his own, and climbed aboard the buttery expanse of her torso. He debated whether or not to tape her mouth, but decided that, if she got noisy, he could shut her up quickly enough.

With the first thrust into her perfumed pussy, Charlie got a surprise. Unlike Deborah Engels and Peggy, who'd been so dry that fucking them was like jerking off into sandpaper, Roxane was moist and hot, like fucking the inside of a buttered biscuit.

As he worked, she moaned and rolled her head luxuriantly from side to side. A spectacular bruise was flowering on her jaw, but her lips were curved into a smile approaching radiance.

"Oh, God," she said. "I came. I came so hard I think I died."

Charlie stopped thrusting.

"You mean...just now?"

"When you hit me, I came like crazy." Wickedness flashed in her blue eyes, as she added, "That's the best orgasm there is, but most men are too chickenshit to hit me hard enough."

"But that ain't possible. I knocked you cold."

"And made me come. Right at that second. It's like an incredible explosion—the blow and the orgasm combined. It's the only way I can come. It's why I started doing the boxing show at the club. I thought...I guess it's silly but...I thought there might be other girls like me and I might meet them. But it didn't turn out like that. Everyone's so scared of getting hurt or hurting someone else that they don't hit hard at all. But you knew what I like, and you don't even know me. How is that?"

The urge to punch her again warred in Charlie with the desire to hear more. Just the fact that she was talking to him, not struggling or begging to be set free, threw his plans off balance.

"I have trouble coming myself," he heard himself say. "It's like I can't let go. Unless I hurt somebody and lately..."

She looked up, apparently unafraid. "Yes?"

"...not even then. Even when I...when I was hurting somebody, the last time I still couldn't get off."

"I'll bet I could make you come."

As she said it, Charlie's eyes went almost involuntarily to the picture of his mother, the agate paperweight of the woman on the pedestal.

Put a woman on a pedestal, treat her like gold.

A surge of hormones and sadism pumped the blood into his hard-on until it felt like the jawbone of a whale.

"Don't need any help," he said, ramming into her pussy with all his weight as he brought his fist around into her cheek. A red welt blossomed under one eye. She sighed and didn't move again for a while, but her cunt stayed just as succulently juicy as before and the blissful look upon her face implied more a contented sleep than unconsciousness.

Charlie fucked her until she came around, but he didn't hit her again. Instead he asked her if she had really gotten off.

"Incredibly. Like rockets." Her breath was coming in little breathy gasps. "My God, I know I'm getting beaten up, but these orgasms are to die for."

Charlie considered this. His cock was a rod of fire, his hips ached from thrusting, and his balls felt like bags of concrete, but as near as he could tell, he was no closer to coming than when he'd started.

"You said you could help me get off. How?"

"You know how. By hitting you, of course. You'd have to let me punch you."

"Aw, come on. You ain't that strong. You couldn't knock me out."

"I wouldn't have to. Just one punch, just so you could let go. That's all it would take. You'd come like you'd never believe."

Roxane's left eye was swelling shut. A trail of blood had meandered from her lower lip and dried along her cheek. She didn't look so foxy anymore, not like anybody you'd want to put up on a pedestal, Charlie thought, but perversely, the worse she looked, the more painfully hard his boner became.

"All right, get up."

She did so, but she was wobbly. When Charlie untied her wrists, she teetered forward, knocking the items on the nightstand, the photo and the paperweight and a stack of *Buxum Bondagettes* to the floor.

"I need my tote bag."

Charlie tossed it to her. She sat on the floor amid the spilled magazines, the bruises on her face contrasting with the ripe, tawny flesh of her body, and began to root around inside the bag.

It occurred to Charlie she might have a gun or a can of Mace in there.

"Hey, I need to see your hands. What've you got in there?"

By way of answer, she threw him one of her boxing gloves. Charlie tossed it up and down a few times, imagining it was her boob, severed from her body but still bouncy, firm. He put the idea away for possible use later on.

When he looked back, she was scrambling around on the floor, hurriedly lacing the other glove onto her right hand. "I need to wear the glove, otherwise when I hit you, I could break my hand."

That brought a grin to Charlie's face—like she thought a broken hand was going to matter when this was over.

"Now hold onto your dick," Roxane said, "and get ready to shoot to the ceiling. If you don't start to come like gangbusters when I pop you, I won't know why not."

Charlie spit into his hand, stroked his stiff rod.

"One punch," he said. "One punch is all you get, and if I don't come just the way you say, then it's my turn, and I'll hurt you, I'll hurt you bad."

"One punch is all I need," she said, and something that felt a lot harder than any fist slammed into the side of Charlie's mouth. His eyes flew open, and she slugged him again, a brutal uppercut that rocked back his head. This time he swayed and flopped onto the bed, arms up to fend her off, but she was on top of him and the thing she'd put inside the glove before she laced it up—stone, a heavy slab of stone, shaped like the bottom of a pedestal, the kind you were supposed to put a woman on—shattered his jaw in two places, and the next blow cracked his cheekbone and the one after that smeared the cartilage of his nose in a ruby stripe across his cheek and...somewhere, far off, beyond the firestorm of pain in his smashed face, he heard Roxane cry out that she was coming.

She had lied to him, though. Not just about hitting him only one time, but about something else, too. It was the last thing in this life that Charlie learned. Because it wasn't at the moment of unconsciousness that he climaxed, but much later, at the point of death, that he came and came.

Making the Woman

D. J. and me, we decided to make us a woman.

One all our own. To look at. Explore.

Not that we haven't seen real ones. We're both twelve and we've seen a *lot*, let me tell you. Our mothers and sisters and aunts, bathing, dressing, fussing in front of the mirror—hypnotized before all that shiny, glittery *girly* stuff, the eye gook, the mascara, the brushes. We've seen them naked, too—squatting on the toilet, stretched out fish-pale and gleaming in the tub, scooping their boobs up into their bras like double dips of vanilla ice cream.

I even saw Mom fucking one time—while Dad was at work.

I'd got sent home from school for fighting. She had a man on the couch with her. I'll never forget how her legs looked, straight up in the air like drumsticks, the feet twitching a little, and the guy's fat, pink butt in between.

And D.J. and I spied on my older sister Charleen and her boyfriend, dry-humping on the living-room floor, making sucky-smacky noises, every now and then getting a glimpse of Charlene's tits while we huddled under the stairs, making gagging faces at each other, but fascinated, too, like at a really gross horror movie that you hate, but then you go back to see it two or three more times. I remember the excitement made my blood feel like carbonated soda, my belly tight as a fist.

Women. They seem so strange, so Other. Aliens pretending to be people, but not quite pulling it off. Always nervous, scared of everything. Be careful, say our mothers and aunts and sisters, don't eat too fast, don't talk to strangers, don't run, don't yell, don't get dirty. *Don't*—it's like the only way they know to start a sentence, and it sucks.

Yech to all that. Not our world. Our world is running and fighting and yelling and not being anything like them, making fun of how they walk and talk and smell. And how they act around the men—the phony sweetness, flirty sexiness—sometimes it creeps me out. It makes me want to hurt them, bite their fannies, pinch their titties, blow boogers out my nose and gross them out.

Plump, soft, scaredy-cats always *doing* stuff to themselves—shave the legs, curl the lashes, wax the mustache—never *doing* unto others, as the Bible (sort of) tells us to, do and do and do to others till they bleed and puke and die.

If it bothers you, the fuck *do* something to somebody else, I say.

So we decided to make us a woman.

Lucas, the ten-year-old retard who lives with his grandma in the housing project 'cross the street, saw D.J. and me headed up the block and wanted to come, too. Fuck that. For one thing, Lucas don't think too good 'cause his Momma drank so much 'fore he got born, she killed most all his brain cells. He's also a nerd—soft and dimply and apple-round, *womanish*. He's even got small jiggly tits you can see under his clothes. His butt's like a plug of raw cookie dough with legs added on. Lucas the Doughboy, we call him.

Eat it, Lucas. Fuck you. Go play with your dolls.

Go bite the tits off your dolls, little boy.

D.J.'s dad used to have a poster of a naked woman in his garage, her body carved up into sections and marked with words like Prime Cut, Shank, Rib Roast. He'd drink Jose Cuervo and brag about the bitches he'd fucked and how women were only good for one thing and not even that after their cunts started farting out babies.

D.J.'s dad is making license plates at the State Farm now, doing two years on a wife-beating charge. When he gets out, D.J.'s mom better not be anywhere around here.

And my old man, he don't live here no more since Mom caught him in the basement taking pictures of Charlene and one of her friends dressed up in all that girly-stuff—garter belts and lace bras and panties slashed for the gash. Kinda makes me sick to my stomach, but I still wish I coulda seen Charlene and her friend with their boobs sticking out, wiggling around in hooker spikes, pretending they were already grown-up women.

I mean, I want to puke thinking about it, but I wish I coulda seen two sluts like that in action.

Where D.J. and I live, only a few of the houses have people livin' in 'em. The rest are broken-down junk houses, roach motels, flophouses for street bums and bag ladies, and cracked-out hookers walkin' stiff-legged like they got a pair of pliers up their cooze.

So the day we decided to make the woman, D.J. swiped some tampons from the Circle-K and I took one of Charlene's hair-pieces and Mom's douche bag, and we headed up to where the buildings are most all empty.

Woulda been nice, I thought, we'da had a beach to go to, soft pale sand scooped up round and firm, make tits and ass, but this neighborhood ain't no California and all we had to make our woman from was dirt.

Plenty of that, though, in the lot behind the empty Rexall Store at the corner of 5th and Pearl. Nobody to see either, dumpsters block the view from up the street.

D.J. used a pocketknife to trace the woman's outline. Big hips, a skinny waist and neck. For boobs, we scooped up fistfuls of dirt and packed them firm, used bottle caps for nipples. I found a clump of weeds and used it for pubic hair. D.J. unwrapped a tampon and stuck it up into the weeds like it was coming out of the woman's snatch. Then we drew a head and stuck on Charlene's blonde wig. I found a crumpled condom, and we used that for the mouth. We both laughed, D.J. and me, till our sides hurt.

I put the douche bag on the woman's head. I wanted to plug a tampon up her ass, too, but she was just an outline in the dirt. She didn't have no backside or no inside or no feelings. She didn't count.

Suddenly I felt so mad I wanted to tear somethin' up.

I picked up a rock and threw it at the woman. "Bitch," I said.

"Cunt," said D.J. and did the same.

"Pussy."

"Slut."

"Whore."

But it wasn't enough. I jumped up and down on the woman's tits. D.J. stomped on her head. Hatred for our woman—for *all* women—spilled out of us like puke.

In the shadows near the dumpsters, I heard something move, picked up another rock.

"Whatchoo guys doing?" said Lucas, ambling into view, gawking at the woman's tits like he was seeing a ten-car pile-up on the interstate. "What's this? Pitcher of a fuck?"

I don't know which one of us threw the first rock. Maybe it was both at once, but a stone hit Lucas in the temple and he oozed down like chocolate melting, and then D.J. bashed him with another as he groveled on the ground, flopped and floundered on top of our woman like he was tryin' to figure out how to fuck her.

"Him!" I shouted, grabbing the knife. "He's our woman!"

We pulled his pants off, yanked down his jockey shorts. He was startin' to thrash around, so D.J. sat on his face and held his arms. I yanked his limp dick up with one hand and—I hesitated. For a second I felt afraid. Then I remembered all the things I'd seen and heard in my twelve years—Dad whippin' Mom's ass and mine, Charlene with a black eye, a broke jaw, courtesy of her boyfriend, and all the words, the words coming like fists, *cunt* and *pussy* and *gash,* and before I'd even thought of all the words I knew for woman, Lucas's dick came loose in my hand. I lifted it up and war-whooped as blood poured from the hole, gushed like a bitch on her period.

Lucas howled.

D.J. leaped up and danced around the blood spigot where Lucas's dick used to be. "Lucas the Dickless Doughboy. Lucas is a woman now!"

"You cunt, you gash, you piece of shit!" I cried, throwing the wet tube of flesh to D.J., who caught it and tossed it high in the air, blood spattering on Lucas's flip-flopping body.

"Bitch!"

"Pussy!"

"Cunt!"

"A girl! A girl!"

"Like us!"

Rush

There are a lot of ways to kill yourself, but the trouble is, most of them hurt. Personally, I never liked hurt. I like death in tiny, titillating increments, like wine sipped from a thimble, shrinking down until I feel like I could slip through a needle's eye while my brain sponges up the blackness and all remaining consciousness pools in the tip of my clit and the friction-sore lips of my pussy.

I like to cum close to the edge.

All it takes is someone with strong hands and no hidden homicidal urges, someone who knows when to stop.

So one night when we're high on retsina and a March rainstorm is tap dancing on *Hornpiper's* decks, pinging off the hatch like birdshot, I tell Boz what I want. He laughs in a kind of effeminate way, which is funny considering the steroids he scarfs down like M&M's have changed him from a short, bearded Greek into a short, bearded Greek built like Hulk Hogan, but I can see the fear twitch across his face like a muscle spasm. I'm not surprised. Like all the other guys I've slept with since Mimi died, the idea of choking as a turn-on freaks him out.

"Look, Fritzy, suppose I get carried away? Then what do I do—dump your body over the side and sail for Caracas?"

"You're not gonna kill me," I say, lighting a smoke on Boz's precious ketch just to see if he lets me get away with it. "You got me off the street, gave me a place to stay after Mimi was murdered. You love me."

"That still don't mean I couldn't kill you."

He has a point, the irony of which isn't lost on me. I tell him I'll take the risk. "All I want is a rush."

Boz reaches over, plucks the cigarette out of my mouth, flings it out the starboard porthole.

"Jesus, Fritzy, you got a death wish, don't you?"

A death wish—maybe that was Mimi's problem, too. When I met her last year, she was pedaling pussy on A1-A along the Fort Lauderdale Strip. I was waiting tables at the Greek Circus, saving money to go back to school at Broward Community College, and dating Boz, who worked for his uncle Stavros as a short-order cook but whose main vocations in life were being a boat-bum and pumping up beefcake at Gold's Gym across the street. The Circus was a hooker haven. Mimi liked to cruise in for baklava and java along about 1 A.M. I needed a friend. She wanted a wife and—more to the point—a piece of pussy.

I was twenty-three, fresh out of a marriage that should have got me on the *Oprah* show, where I could've talked about being married to a cracker who beat me up for infractions like buying the wrong kind of fishing lures. I'd never been outside the state of Florida, spent all my life in Citrus Springs, until the night I packed my bag after one split lip too many and took a bus to Fort

Lauderdale. Now I was just trying to hold onto my job and fend off the scuzzball clientele without forfeiting my tips.

I was also dumb as dirt.

Mimi, for example, fascinated me, with her macho strut and studded leathers and her way of staring at me up and down, the way a man would do. I thought fucking for money sounded dark and dangerous and liberated as shit. A sexual bungee jump.

One night when I said something to that effect, Mimi invited me back to her apartment just off the Strip and set me straight. First off, she pointed out the crooked little bump at the bridge of her nose, which I'd thought was kind of handsomely Semitic, but turned out to be a parting present from her first (and only) pimp. Then she wriggled out of her pink spandex tights and showed me a rump polka-dotted with scar tissue, courtesy of a freak who hummed Roy Orbison tunes while he tortured her with cigarettes.

Okay. So hooking wasn't exactly what *Pretty Woman* made it out to be. It was still exotic and forbidden. Mimi's scars seemed like wounds suffered in some covert and undeclared war that the Pricks had waged against women since time began. A war in which my ex-husband—and before him, my father—had been bucking for officer status. I figured Mimi and I were both decorated veterans, long overdue for R&R. But when she kissed me that first time, it wasn't tender like I'd expected, but rough and hard, like the start of a date rape.

"Go in the bathroom and wash up," she said. "You smell like your greasy Greek boyfriend."

When I came out, she'd put on a satiny kimono and lay reclined seductively upon the couch.

"Understand that if we're going to do this," she said, "we're going to do it my way."

And we always did. Somehow that made it more exciting.

It was Mimi who taught me about the rush. First time she wound the sash of her kimono around my neck, I thought, *She's kidding, right?* But then she leaned above me, all creamy curves, and as she gently, lovingly, tightened the sash, the bed began to plummet, and Mimi uncapped the poppers and held them under my nose with one hand while she starved my brain for blood by twisting the sash with the other. After that, there was no bed, but only a pulsing, black-red tunnel, the view a sperm might get rocketing through a menstruating pussy, and, just at the brink, I came and passed out, not caring—for that moment—if I woke up or not.

After that it was like I had a hard-on for death—and for Mimi—all the time.

Doing things "Mimi's way" involved a lot of changes. I broke up with Boz, quit my job at the Greek Circus, and moved into Mimi's place. Our arrangement was as old-fashioned as Ozzie and Harriet. Mimi the older breadwinner who called the shots, me the little wifey homemaker. For a pair of pussy-eaters, we had family values that would have done the Brady Bunch proud. I felt like I belonged to someone. Like I had a home where I could close the door behind me and feel safe. A home where I didn't have a husband rubbing my face in the food if it wasn't cooked to his taste or a father who, starting when I was twelve, liked to stick his fingers up my cunt to see if I was still a virgin. The only part of our arrangement that I hated was when I'd come home and find the door to the guest bedroom shut, fucky-sucky sounds coming from within. My imagination would get to flying like a blender on puree. I'd go into the kitchen, get out the bread board and the carving knife and—*thwack*—stab my fucking father in the eye or—*thwack*—slash my husband's throat—killing them in time to Mimi's faked moans.

I hear a decidedly real moan slide from my own lips now, thinking about the night that Mimi died.

"At least try it, Boz."

In the moonlight slanting through the porthole, Boz's belly looks hard and plated as the topside of a gator. His long hair falls across his face and into mine. He glides inside. Smooth hard strokes, like spikes driven into my pussy, nailing me to the bunk, kisses that drive my lips back into my teeth.

I take his hand, guide it to my throat.

Do it.

He starts to squeeze, but does it wrong. Puts pressure on my larynx. Hurts like a crowbar across the windpipe. Worse, makes me sputter, choke like someone whose prime rib went down the wrong way. Hurts like hell. I don't like hurt.

Goddamn it, Boz.

I move his hand so his fingers are pressing either side of my neck just under the jaw, the place where you can cut the blood flow to the brain by pressing on the carotid arteries. Now he's got it. Time for the ride. Sink, sink with the strokes, each thrust pounding me deeper into the bed while my brain blurs and dims and thoughts dissolve, grainy memories of a grainy life getting vaguer, smudgier. Men lined up like tenpins, my husband, father, Mimi's johns all merging into faceless fucks. Domino men, they topple into one another, knock each other flat with their erections, clack, clack, clack, as I fall—down until—Boz stops. "I'm sorry, Fritzy. This choking stuff don't turn me on."

You fucking pussy wuss.

The rage that rises in me is punctuated by a crash, as though my anger's metamorphosed into a gremlin stumbling around on deck.

"The fuck was that—?"

Boz executes a spectacular leap, the air farting from my pussy as he scrabbles in the bedside drawer where he keeps the KY and the Vaseline.

I blink to clear my vision, see a silver snub-nosed .22 poking out of Boz's fist as he flattens himself behind the door, makes a sign to me to be quiet. This wasn't how I planned to die, in some kind of dockside shoot-out, but if it must be, let it be now, while I'm too aroused and angry to be scared.

"Hey, Boz, man, I knocked on the hatch, you in there or what?"

"Fuck you, Chess, we were ballin'. I thought you was a fuckin' burglar."

Boz lowers the .22, stalks back to the bunk as Chessman descends the ladder.

"Next time you come aboard my boat unannounced," says Boz, "I'll blow your balls out your fuckin' asshole."

The image cracks me up, even though I know Boz's tough

talk is mostly for my benefit. In reality, Chessman is his connection for the steroids that keep those mammoth muscles from deflating like little saggy tits, and Boz would rather kiss his ass than waste it. Although, personally, I could scrub Chessman's innards off the floorboards with a toothbrush and find it rewarding work.

Chessman used to visit Mimi when he came around the Strip, selling steroids to the gay muscle boys. She said his life's ambition was to be a pimp and that you could make sandwich spread from the cheese underneath his foreskin.

"Hey, fuck it, Boz, you'll be glad to see me when I show you what I got."

He comes over to the bunk, ignoring me like I'm a pattern on the bedspread—split-beaver percale—and dumps his latest goods out for Boz's inspection. I crawl back into my shorts and T-shirt, suddenly cold. Breeze blowing in the hatch creeps up my legs, salty tentacles of cold flap around my ankles clammy as a mummy's gauzes.

"Look, you got your Danocrine, your Anabol. Give you thighs like Trigger, man."

Boz examines the bottles like each pill was a precious stone. I can see Chessman's intrusion is already history. "Get you the cash," he says and heads toward the aft cabin. Which leaves Chessman and me alone. He grins and skins me with his eyes, then moves closer, treating me to a view of the boner tenting up his jeans. His odor mingles all the stenches of a wharfside tavern—beer and piss and eau de rut.

"So, Fritzy, you went and got one o' them dyke cuts, huh?" he says, eyeing my newly acquired punk do. Mimi liked to wind my long hair around her fingers, tug me along like a dog on a very short lease. I couldn't cut off the memories, so I cut the hair. "Yeah, real butch," Chessman goes on. "You still in mournin' for your girlfriend or maybe Boz just ain't man enough to give you what you want?"

"He gives me plenty. With enough left over for your mother, Chessman."

"Yeah? Well, my mother's a whore like you, so I'm sure she'd love it." He shrugs. "Sure hope Boz remembers to use protection. You look like walkin' HIV to me."

Boz comes back in, hands money to Chessman, who counts it and frowns like he's fighting to squeeze out the world's largest turd.

"Hey, man, what's this—this ain't enough—"

"It's all I got right now. Health department closed the Circus down for code violations two weeks last month. I didn't get paid."

Chessman grumbles, "Hey, fuck this shit, you need another job." They head topside, spilling more wind down the hatch, scent of dried seaweed, dead fish, and brine. I hear Chessman say something like "ought to turn her skinny ass out" and Boz tells him to keep it down.

I snuggle up into the sheets and think maybe Boz does love me, for real, because I'm not sleek and cut like the bodybuilder chicks he works out with at Gold's or curvy plush like Mimi was. I'm thin and nervous, and Boz doesn't let me look for work. He says he likes for me to be here on *Hornpiper,* because he loves me I suppose (like Mimi loved me?), and that last idea's so funny that I cry myself to sleep.

A little later, Boz flips me over, hard-on headed home.

"Fritzy, you know Chessman's got a thing for you. You ever want to, you know, fuck him, it'd be okay."

I think I heard Boz say that. I hope not. I hope I only dreamed it.

I pretend like I'm asleep, let Boz go on without me.

Thursday is the six-month anniversary of Mimi's death. I can't sleep, sit up sipping that licorice-tasting ouzo Boz steals from work, listening to the wind rattling the rigging like a fractious ghost. The homicide detective who investigated Mimi's death figured it was one of her johns that did her, wrapped the scarf so tight around her neck it bruised the flesh.

I didn't tell him Mimi liked that kind of scene, that she could play the top or bottom with equal zeal. Why bother? Straights just laugh at SM, got no respect for kink, the intensity of pleasure on both sides. Control and helplessness, dominance and passivity, it's more than just the bodies fucking, Mimi used to say, it's the minds, the souls.

Along about three inches down the bottle, I start thinking maybe if I do like Mimi did, try the streets again myself, I'll find someone to kill me, too (Hey, mister, do you date?). By accident, of course. *I didn't mean to, officer, things got out of control. She wanted me to choke her. Begged me to. Said it was the rush she wanted. I told her I don't do that SM shit, no sir, not me, but then, once I got started...*

Around five, I crawl into the bunk with Boz. It's chilly and damp, and I feel about four years old inside and even almost miss my father in a crazy kind of way. Forget the streets. If I'm gonna die, I want to die at the hands of someone who loves me. That's the way it ought to be, you know. I fall asleep wondering if Boz qualifies.

Love—what a fucking, cruel, four-letter word. I was so sure Mimi loved me. The best times with her, the times I felt the safest and securest, were right after sex, when I'd cuddle in her arms and she'd tell me stories, and I'd feel like her little girl. I know now they were lies. At the time, though, I believed her, thought we were planning out our future like any other couple. She'd talk about her sister who ran a daycare center in Houston, said maybe she'd give up the life, we'd move to Houston, start over, join this church she'd heard about that marries gays and lesbians. Maybe one of us could go get knocked up at a sperm bank so we could start a family.

"You'd marry me, wouldn't you, Fritzy?"

And I'd feel embarrassed at the happy-silly smile on my face and the glow in my gut as I said yes.

"You'd have a kid with me?"

Then I had to tell her what I'd never had the nerve to tell my husband, that I couldn't have kids. My old man's elbow-deep inspections to make sure of my virginity had scarred up my insides so bad a doctor told me I'd never be able to have children.

It was the only time I ever let Mimi see me cry.

Telling Mimi about my father gave her an idea that she'd elaborate on whenever she got loaded. About how we'd drive out to Houston, take our time, hit the honkytonks and truck stops and murder a few johns along the way.

"It'd be easy. Two women with a car. We hang out at a truck stop, show some tit. Get us a trick in the car, one sucks him while the other softens his head up with a tire iron. Cut him up and dump him in a ditch, throw his dick out the window fifty miles up the road, then drive on and do it again. Like them two women in that road movie, only we don't drive off no cliff at the end."

And we'd both roll around on the bed together laughing.

I'd curl against her, face smothered in the breasts I loved to nurse from. I understood then why men have tit fixations, fall in love with big-bosomed earth mother types.

"Would you come to Houston with me, Fritzy?"

(Lying cunt.)

"Sure."

"Would you help me kill some tricks?"

(Like it was easy as planning a bake sale.)

"Sure, if I get to cut the dicks off."

On Friday night, Boz gets fired from the Circus. I offer to go ask for my old waitress job back, but he says no, he wants me here on *Hornpiper*. Wants me at home. His nerves are shot, he's been out of steroids now for weeks, and I can see him sometimes flexing in the mirror, studying for shrinkage like a woman worried that her cleavage isn't what it used to be.

And Chessman hasn't been around, which must mean Boz is seriously broke.

Below deck, it smells of beer and sex, a boat too long at port, languishing in the doldrums. I want to motor out of the Intercoastal into the Atlantic, unfurl *Hornpiper*'s main and mizzen and jib, pick up some breeze, head for Bimini, but when I ask him, Boz says no. We can't go anyplace, he says. We got to wait.

"You want to screw?"

"Just wait," he says, sounding a lot like my ex-husband as he goes topside to check the sky.

So I tidy up the galley and dream about the trip Mimi and I were going to make to Houston, dicks flung from the windows like banana peels, and suddenly—as if the ferocity of my thoughts has somehow reached his groin—Boz is back, pushing me onto the bunk, stripping off my bathing suit bottom.

"I want you."

Finally. Relief washes through me. Boz still loves me, still wants to fuck. I can't believe I still get the two confused. After Mimi, I should have learned.

He enters me so quickly I have no time to lubricate, feel dry, searing pain as I'm rent.

"You like this, Fritzy, don't you?"

Something creaking, not the bunk.

He grips my throat, no-nonsense now, starts squeezing like he wants to push my tonsils past my wisdom teeth.

White fizz behind my eyes. Confetti vision.

Movement on deck…I'm sure now.…

"I know you want this, Fritzy. Tell me you want it."

My pelvis answers, arching up to match his thrust. I'm slick with want now, but his hands are too impatient, pushing me down into a midnight sea, moonless and starless, tiny silver-spangled fish darting through inky water, deeper now, where nothing lives, no fish, no light, and *Hornpiper* upended, sinking down, a phantom vessel carrying me under, and just as I'm about to come, Mimi ruins it—Mimi's voice telling me to get the hell out of her apartment, she doesn't love me, never did, she's met someone, a man, and Mimi's face, terrified and mute, gapes up at me as I wrap a scarf around her neck and choke her into loving me.

Mercifully, Boz's hands push me deeper, beyond memory, out of Mimi's reach.

Do it, do it, do it.

Mimi, damn you, stay dead.

She does, and, for a long moment, I'm dead with her.

Bad dream. Shit.

The weight's all wrong.

Not Mimi.

Not Boz, either.

The rhythm, too. Not Boz's. My pussy knows.

Oh, shit, oh shit, oh Boz, you didn't, no.

"Hey man, this ain't half-bad for a dead piece. She starts to come around, how about I choke her out again? Give you another week's supply of Anovar."

And Boz: "Hey, hurry up, man."

"Thought you was gonna turn her out. Put her ass to work."

"I am. Just give me time."

It's dark as death in the cabin, which helps when I start reaching for the drawer. Also the fact that Chessman's close to coming, convulsing into the kind of spasms that usually cause bystanders to shove something in the person's mouth so they don't bite their tongue in half.

I do that, too, but it's not a tongue depressor.

At this range, I can't miss. The explosion from the .22 shaves off Chessman's mustache and most of his nose. Funny thing, the eyes stay open. I see them, bugging, bulging, as he flies backward, dick still hard as he pops out of me, cum dribbling between my legs.

"The fuck—Fritzy—"

Boz gets it in the groin. A dickless Boz would be better off dead. I aim a clean shot through the left eye, watch putty-colored sludge freckle the map of the Intercoastal Waterway behind Boz's head.

And I come. Come so hard you'd think I was flicking my clit instead of the trigger.

Gotta be cool now. Like after I did Mimi. Wipe the prints off the gun, get my shit together. Get the hell outta here.

Roid rage, boys. Musta been it.

The Strip hasn't changed a whole lot since I've been away. Topless joints, wet T-shirt contests, girl pussy, boy pussy, doesn't make much difference what you put it in, long as you put it someplace.

I hate that scene, so I hit the highway, hitchhiking, Houston-bound. Lady-in-distress. My car broke down a ways up the road. My boyfriend and I had a fight, he kicked me out of the car.

Once in their car: "Hey honey, do you date?"

They date. Almost all of them do and the ones that don't I talk into it. And while they unholster their dicks, I pull out my

.22 caliber cock and fuck them first. And when the bullet puts a pussy right between their eyes, I get the wildest rush.

Better than I got from Mimi. Better than from Boz.

There are a lot of ways to get a rush.

There are a lot of ways to kill people, too, but almost all of them hurt.

Personally, I don't give a fuck.

The Safety of Unknown Cities

Someday you'll come to love this. Those were the words the jailer said when she clicked on the chain. The chain was secured to a leg of the bed, and the bed was of heavy oak. The prisoner wasn't strong enough to lift it.

The jailer held a threaded needle which she had sterilized in boiling water in the kitchen.

It's just a game, the jailer said.

And began to sew.

The prisoner screamed and begged and made promises

of future perfection, future obedience to any and all rules.

The jailer reminded the prisoner that she had run away before and would likely do that again—and more besides—if given the opportunity.

Still, the prisoner cried bitterly, so the jailer took her in her arms and held her, stroked her, kissed her, touching her in places where she both dreaded touch and craved it.

Thus soothed, she finally tumbled into fitful sleep.

Someday you'll come to love this, said the jailer. *Someday you'll understand.*

The prisoner was nine years old.

In early fall in the city of Hamburg, Val Petrillo arrived late for a slave auction. It was held in the basement of Das K, one of Europe's most notorious sex clubs, and consisted of nude or seminude men and women, willing participants all, being auctioned off for an hour or two of use in one of the private rooms in the establishment.

Val had heard about the auction—and about a particular "slave"—only hours before and had interrupted a weekend tryst with a Japanese businessman to fly in from Geneva.

It was her first visit to Hamburg, and she regretted the necessity of rushing directly from the airport to the club. Such untoward haste was not her style. She liked to savor a city at leisure and at length, to arrive by train, preferably with the sun just coming up and to sit by herself on the platform for a few minutes, observing the purposeful strides of the commuters, the slink and slouch of the derelicts and whores, the foreign tourists, often timid and unsure, and trying not to look so, but uncertain of the language or the proper direction in which to forge, and feeling their way with caution in an alien terrain. Val never considered herself part of this joyful, seedy, bubbling throng, but rather a distant watcher, the way a pigeonkeeper might observe the milling, shitting, shuffling of the flock.

Sometimes in such a moment of private observation, she'd see a particularly striking face, an eye-catching shape of hand or jaw, a memorable breast or ankle and, if the watched one happened to look back, a brief moment of meeting, of connection might occur, and Val would think, "You might have been my sister, brother, friend for life. You might have been my lover."

Sometimes such people did become her lovers, but the beauty promised in that first gaze never quite matched Val's expectations, no more than the skylines of the cities that she visited, some gleaming, thrusting ornate minarets or towering slabs of glass proudly into the sky, others squat and shabby or drab with soot and the grit of harbored pestilence, ever quite lived up to her dreams.

So she stayed on the move. From city to city, bed to bed. Indulging her two addictions. Wanderlust and fleshlust. The passions of her life. Over the past few months, however, a new purposefulness had infused Val's journeying. In the sex parlors and private clubs she frequented, she'd begun to hear strange rumors. Occasionally, from a pair of lips made slack by drink or satiation, she'd heard whispered tales of a place she'd dreamed about but not yet visited, a carnal city of such perversion that it tested sanity, a place beside which the fleshpot Sodoms and modern-day Gomorrahs of the known world paled by comparison.

Always the teller of the tale was vague in his or her allusions, but more than once she'd heard tell of a man known only as the Turk. It was he, so the rumormongers claimed, who could offer entrance to the City.

It was in pursuit of the Turk then, be he real or the fabrication of minds too corrupted by venality to know truth from lies, that Val had come to Das K. A young man from the Philippines, an unskilled laborer who loaded and unloaded cargo on the Hamburg docks by day and indulged his taste for SM by night, was scheduled to be "auctioned off" in a few minutes. Word had it that he had met the Turk, had even ventured to the City. Intrigued, Val was intent on meeting him.

In her early thirties, Val was a slender woman with black hair curtaining a tanned and oval face and features sufficiently symmetrical and absent of expression to make her, if not quite conventionally beautiful, at least inscrutable. Edgy with anticipation, she sat alone now at a back table of the club, sipping Courvoisier. A pair of twins, two young Nigerian women with enormous flaring nostrils and lips the size of dark red rose petals, were being auctioned off, sold at last to an older, professorial type in bifocals and tweed.

A blonde young woman, leashed and corsetted, was purchased by a leather dyke, who handcuffed her prize before leading her off the stage. Then a man, all strut and beefcake, with a complex lacery of green tattoos entwining his arms and thighs in a kind of epidermal kudzu, was sold for an outrageous price to a flamboyant creature with sequins in her false eyelashes and a bulge in the crotch of her spandex tights.

When the Philippino boy was finally brought on stage, Val let the bidding rise, then quickly bid a sum so large no one ventured to try to top her. As she was going to the cashier to pay before collecting her slave, Val felt herself observed. Turning slowly, she saw a platinum-haired young man with green lynx eyes watching her from the bar. He wore a silk shirt and loose-fitting black satin vest, a diamond earring and ghoul eyeliner that would have shamed a whore. His flesh was so pale it looked translucent, a stitching together of gossamer insect wings. When their eyes met, he raised his drink, a tiny cordial glass containing what appeared to be a gold liqueur and pantomimed a toast. Val gave him no acknowledgement. Pretty though he was, at the moment, she had no use for any but her purchase.

Minutes later, alone with her slave, Val quickly forgot the hauntingly pale features of the apparition at the bar. She took the Philippino boy, whose name the auctioneer informed her was Santos, to an upstairs whipping room, where she initiated the proceedings by stripping and ordering the slave to fuck her. He did so with might and gusto, but after a few minutes, Val feigned displeasure and secured Santos's wrists to a pair of manacles affixed to one wall. Then, availing herself of the sturdiest of a selection of whips, she beat the boy's naked back and buttocks until his glossy, nut-brown flesh was a tapestry of raised pink welts.

Through it all, the slave uttered not a sound, which disappointed Val somewhat, as she found the chief reward of flogging to be the moans and cries of a submissive, and so she wielded the whip with greater vigor but managed to wring forth not one plea or cry.

At length, she freed Santos's hands and allowed him to fuck her to climax, her own and his, which he accomplished with much writhing and shuddering but not a single sound. They lay still for a while then, breathing the heady, pungent odors of orgasm, hearing laughter and applause from the auction still continuing downstairs.

"I heard about you in Switzerland," Val began in German, one hand covering and idly petting Santos's cock. "I've been told you're quite the connoisseur of perversions."

He smiled and shrugged. It occurred to Val that perhaps he spoke no German. She tried English then, with no better results. Summoning up what meager Spanish she possessed, Val persevered, "Is it true you've had relations with a man known as the Turk? And that you've been to a place they call the City?"

Again, that small apologetic smile, but this time Val knew he'd understood. His penis, when she uttered the words "the Turk" had stiffened beneath her hand.

"You're still my slave, you know. And I asked you…"

Santos leaned forward, pressed his full mouth to hers. His lips parted. Val entered him with her tongue, probing, thrusting, then…

She pulled back, skin goosefleshing, with a cry of dismay.

Santos grinned at her, opened his mouth wide for her inspection. His mouth was empty, a vacant cave, the stump of tongue a grey cauterized root deep in his throat. He gave a gurgling, half-formed sound, a kind of muffled oink.

Scarcely flinching, Val snatched up her handbag and dug out a pen and paper. "Answer my questions," she commanded. "Write it down."

Santos held the pen as if it were a foreign object. At the top of the page, he scrawled an "X." Val asked again and got the same response. The boy was either illiterate or pretending to be so. His cock, however, was far more communicative. Fully erect now, it pressed lewdly against Val's belly. She slapped the offending piece of meat aside and began to dress.

Santos would tell her nothing, and she was furious. But in another way, she realized, perhaps he'd told her more than she really cared to know. That made her even angrier and, perversely, more anxious than ever before to see the City.

"You didn't keep him very long. He must have disappointed you."

One green lynx eye winked at her above a full mouth uptilted at one corner with bemusement: the pretty young thing from the bar. He'd come up beside her when she left the club and fallen into step.

"He was fine," Val said. "Quite worth what I paid."

"Except he's maimed."

"Not where it counts."

"Unless you purchased him more for what you hoped he'd say than what he'd do."

"I didn't buy the boy for conversation."

"Oh, didn't you?"

Val stopped. They were walking along a narrow street, still in the St. Pauli district, but a good mile north of the Reeperbahn's famed glitz—all neon, sizzle, and glare—and a hundred years away in atmosphere. Here, winding cobbled streets converged and serpentined, dead-ended and then reemerged, a medieval maze of narrow, gabled houses illuminated by pale cones of incandescent light thrown by iron streetlamps. Alone, Val had been content to wander, even at this hour. Now she considered summoning a taxi and going back to the hotel where she'd left the overnight bag with the few belongings she'd seen fit to bring from Geneva. Tomorrow perhaps she would fly back, resume her tryst with her Nagasaki Romeo, assuming he'd not found other company himself.

She turned and stared into those feline eyes, darkly flecked with green and amber.

"Who are you?"

"Majeed," the boy said, extending a pale, long-fingered hand which Val ignored.

"Why are you following me?"

"I'm not following you. I only thought perhaps I might offer you what Santos, with his unfortunate speech impediment, could not. I know you came here seeking information about the City. It's possible that I could help. But now I see I'm only bothering you. You want a hard cock like your little slave's, and here I'm offering you merely words. I'll leave. I wouldn't wish to force my company on you."

He turned to go and Val let him—for six paces. Then curiosity overcame her pride and she called out, "Wait. You're right. I didn't come to Das K for a hard cock. I came for information."

As it turned out, however, Majeed apparently had both. Val took note of the bulge in the tight jeans, sculpted to the youth's body. Majeed told her he had an apartment merely blocks away, but when they arrived, his "home" turned out to be a dilapidated hotel, the kind where rooms are rented by the hour and the sheets are blotchy with questionable stains.

"You will come in with me?" Majeed pulled Val into the shadows. He slid a hand behind her neck, pressed his mouth to hers, enticing her with a lithe tongue made all the more erotic by its equivalent's repulsive absence in her most recent lover's mouth. The boy smelled of musk and cloves, his lips flavored with the lingering trace of mint liqueur. He sucked and nibbled Val's lower lip as one would suck the pulp from a slice of citron.

Val reached down to massage the sweet protuberance at Majeed's groin, but he took her hand away, kissed the perfumed wrist and palm and laid it on his shoulder.

"You aren't afraid?" he said. "To go late at night to the room of a man you barely know?"

Val scrutinized those subtly slanted eyes. She'd been with dangerous men before; it was, in fact, her preference. She'd taken chances all her life and was not about to change her habits now.

"There's only one thing I really fear," she said, "and that's not being free to do what the fuck I please."

Majeed laughed. "Oh really? So what if I were to shackle you to the bed and walk away? Just leave?"

"That might be exciting."

"And if I never came back?"

"You would."

Majeed unlocked the outer door to his derelict abode. They crossed an inner courtyard to a second door which Majeed unlocked, then ascended three flights of stairs. The room into which he ushered Val smelled of herbs and incense, the heady fragrance of decaying temples, untended gardens. The narrow bed was made up with a brocade spread worn thin in places, its gold fringe trailing upon a grimy floor. Scant decoration. On the walls a crucifix; in the windowsills, a treasure trove of incense burners in every shape and size: a gold Buddha and cloisonné-style jar, a terra-cotta pagoda. Majeed selected one and lit an incense stick. The room filled with cloying fragrance, orchids past their prime or rotting camellias.

"So you know about the City?" Val began. "Is it even half-true what I've heard, that Sodom and Gomorrah would seem places of sweet innocence and childlike games by comparison?"

"Not having visited either Sodom or Gomorrah, I wouldn't know."

"But you *have* visited the City?"

"Perhaps. Or maybe I'm just another drugged-out sicko suffering delusions."

"Either way, you must have some tasty stories."

"Which I will tell you," said Majeed, "but first, lie down with me."

Fondly, with neither undue haste nor passion, he began disrobing her. Val allowed it, finding in the movements of the boy's long fingers a mesmerizing languor. As he undressed her, Majeed kissed her neck and eyelids, her nipples and the cleft, still moist from Santos's use, between her legs. His tongue flicked and traced the plump curves of flesh from her clit to the puckered bud between her buttocks.

"Now you," said Val. Kneeling, she unzipped Majeed, whose heavy, uncut cock lolled out into her mouth. She peeled back the foreskin, rimmed and licked the velvet head before swallowing the length of it.

Majeed had still made no move toward taking off his clothes. Perhaps, as he had undressed her, he wished to be undressed himself, Val thought. She stood up and began unfastening the buttons of his vest. Pulling this off, she commenced with the shirt itself, working open half a dozen tiny pearl buttons until she could fold back the silk—to reveal a pair of breasts bound tightly to Majeed's chest by a bra designed to minimize.

Val had seen transsexuals before, but had never partnered one. She hadn't expected this oddity of Majeed. She tried not to show her surprise, but it must have registered on her face for Majeed was smiling, enjoying—as he must always savor it—the look on a new lover's face when he unveiled himself.

Val rolled the tight bra up and over Majeed's head. His breasts were unexpectedly full, with small nipples rouged as dark as strawberries. Val sucked one into her mouth. Majeed moaned and arched his back.

"You're a man on his way to becoming a woman?"

Majeed laughed and pulled her down with him onto the bed. "Guess again."

"A woman on her way—*well* on her way—to becoming a man?"

"Neither."

"Then…"

"Why don't you finish undressing me?"

Val stooped to remove Majeed's shoes and socks. He lifted narrow hips while she tugged down his jeans. His erection bobbed. At the base: two small but perfectly formed testicles. Behind those, where in most men the perineum would be, a moist and parted slit shaved hairless as an egg. It gaped at Val, a single eye, defined by pink and fleshy lids.

"A vagina." Val gazed in wonder at this miracle. She touched the fleshy, dangling labia, then inserted a finger inside Majeed's cunt. He contracted inner muscles, seized and squeezed.

And laughed again, causing breasts and cock to wobble in jarring juxtaposition.

In all her wandering, all her years of sex in strange places among foreign people, Val had never before encountered such a creature. Now, confronted with this marvel, she felt both aroused and awestruck.

"You're splendid," she told Majeed. "Unlike anything I've ever seen."

"Any*one* you've ever seen," Majeed corrected her. "I'm not a freak, you understand, though some people think me one. I'm a hermaphrodite."

"When you were born, your parents…what did they…?"

"They were appalled, to say the least. They said I was a monster, or so I'm told, and sent me to a home in Lexington for freaks and retards."

"And since then?"

"I've lived as a man. I could have an operation to make me more conventional—a chop job or a stitch job, as it were—but I was born like this. I'll die like this. But in the meantime, I prefer to be a male."

"Why is that?"

"It's the females that fall in love, isn't that usually the case? I don't need that weakness."

Val gazed up into eyes as emerald as the towers of Oz. "So you'll be a man tonight?"

"As always."

Majeed lay back upon the bed. Val mounted him. Grinding her hips upon his cock, she reached back to fingerfuck his pussy. She bent forward; their breasts met and mashed together as she sucked on Majeed's lips and sent her tongue exploring the crevices and contours of his mouth.

They made love in all the ways and combinations that Majeed's wondrous anatomy allowed. For the first time in months, Val was able—for a little while—to forget about the City. For surely in Majeed she'd found a prize to please a sultan, the dream-lover of all who hunger for the novel, the bizarre, and yes, Val thought, the freakish, too. Despite his protestations, Majeed was unquestionably a freak, though one of unsurpassing elegance and beauty and, yes, femaleness, too.

To take Majeed's erect cock in her mouth, then dip below and lap and tongue-fuck his pussy was a dizzying excursion into androgyny. To reach up to squeeze those silky breasts while the owner of those breasts drove his cock into her throat, these were pleasures beyond all Val's experience, Majeed's strange beauty an intoxicant of the most seductive sort.

They lay together afterward, hermaphrodite and woman, in a sidelong embrace, genitals still locked together in a gentle clench. From the courtyard down below footsteps sounded. They drew nearer, ascending the inner stairs, and approached along the apartment corridor.

Although his face bore no change of expression, Val could feel

Majeed's muscles tense. His cock, well-drained, slid out of her with a soft smacking sound.

"Don't make a sound," Majeed whispered.

The footsteps stopped outside the door.

Val's head was still on Majeed's breast. She could hear his heart tripling its pace. She held her breath.

"Majeed?" The voice was teasingly seductive and well modulated, a foreign-sounding voice that twisted with difficulty around the German sounds. "Majeed, my love, I know you're in there."

The doorknob turned, but the door was both deadbolted and chained.

The voice dropped to a near whisper and said with renewed cajolery, "Open the door, you little cunt."

There was something about the voice that made Val's heart commence a sprint into her gorge. It was too soft, too honeyed, the voice of a corrupt priest saying prayers while fondling an acolyte in the confessional. And its persuasiveness reached entrails deep, for even as a part of her was terrified, there was another part longing to unlock the door.

"Come on, you pretty little turd. Unlock the door and show me what you've brought home to desecrate tonight. You know how much I like to watch you whore around. So let me in, and I won't hurt you too much."

Val looked at Majeed, who'd gone bone white and appeared almost spellbound with terror. For some reason, she had the feeling that the talk outside the door was some kind of game, that had the owner of the voice desired to, he could have broken the door open without a moment's pause.

"You piece of cum-encrusted shit, you worthless bitch! You know this will only make me hurt you worse when I next see you. And I *will* see you again. You can't run from me. You *need* me. You can't survive without me."

Those last words scared Val most of all, for something in Majeed's entranced stare argued for their veracity. Nor did she expect the sweet-voiced brute beyond the door to leave peacefully. She was sure that in another instant the door would be kicked in.

But no blow came. There was silence for a few minutes, the would-be intruder evidently remaining where he was, listening no doubt, for signs of someone inside the room. To Val this ticking quiet was far more ominous than taunts and threats. The idea of someone lurking in silence just outside the door, pretending not to be there but waiting for a chance to pounce or plotting his next move, aroused long-buried terrors. Her phobia of being trapped slid into consciousness like a stiletto blade parting fat and muscle. She lay motionless in Majeed's trembling embrace, but she could feel the old fears swirling and spiraling around her, rising up to fill her chest, her throat, her mind, like flood waters above a drowned village.

"You little trick, I know you're there. Go ahead and have your fun tonight, but when I come back for you, you'll pay and pay until you can't stop screaming."

The footfalls, a soft and shuffling tread, receded along the corridor.

Val breathed again. She leaped out of bed and crouched down below the windowsill, ignoring Majeed's protests. Presently, a figure emerged into the courtyard, a man in late middle age, tall and stooped, almost emaciated, but with a lush mane of jet hair threaded through with white that fell around his shoulders.

"Get down!" Majeed hissed.

The man crossing the courtyard paused and turned, directing his gaze toward the window through which Val peered. The room was dark, the courtyard lit with moon. She was sure he couldn't see her, and yet, she felt a frisson of both dread and longing, repugnance mixed with lust, as his eyes turned in her direction.

For an instant, just before he turned away again, she experienced the tang of want and craven need: it chilled her utterly.

"Goddamn it, don't let him see you!"

"It's all right. His back is turned. He's leaving."

Majeed cleared his throat, as though reaching for an offhand way to phrase his question, and said, "What does he look like?"

"What do you mean 'what does he look like'? Don't you know?"

"Sometimes he wears…disguises."

"Well, tonight he looks like one of those carved saints from the Day of the Dead in Mexico. Like he doesn't eat enough and never loves."

"Yes," sighed Majeed, as though that description were all too familiar to him.

"Who is he?"

"Just someone I've had some business dealings with."

"What's his name?"

"Why do you care?"

"I want to know."

"Dominick Filakis."

"Your pimp?"

Majeed did not reply, but got out of bed and put a fresh stick of sandalwood in one of the incense burners on the sill. In the gray, rain-washed light of coming dawn, Val could see the ridges of his spine bisecting broad shoulders and tapered waist, the incongruous silhouette of full breasts as he turned again to face her.

"You're a prostitute," said Val.

"You say that like it surprises you."

"Very little surprises me."

"Then you haven't looked hard enough."

The room filled with scents of sandalwood and strawberries that mingled with the smell of sex to form a heady musk. Majeed slid back into the bed, pressed his persimmon lips to Val's.

"Don't worry. I'm not going to charge you. You're not a trick."

"Why not?"

"You asked about the City. Not many people even know about it, and fewer still want to go there. They value life too much."

Val breathed in semen, musk, and flowers. She reached up, tongued Majeed's closed eyes. "Life hasn't got much value if it isn't lived. I lost a big part of my life a long time ago, and I'll never get it back. I made a vow to live what's left me to my own satisfaction."

Majeed sighed. "Spoken like a true Lost Child. One who never had a childhood."

"You could say that."

"You'll have to tell me about it."

"I don't think so."

"But we're going to be together, aren't we? That is, if you still want to see the City."

Val felt her pulse and heartbeat quicken. Her mind spun an erotic web—of decadence past imagining, depravities beyond the capacity of the mind to comprehend, and those few elect, the connoisseurs of flesh who would endure anything in order to experience everything.

"I'm leaving for the City tomorrow," Majeed said.

"You mean today?" said Val, nodding toward the window, where meager flecks of light managed to penetrate the shade, illuminated the cobra shape of scented smoke arising from the incense burner.

"Today, yes, after we get some sleep."

"Filakis, will he come back?"

"Not today," Majeed said, cat-stretching with a languid ease. "He has others to police. I'm small fry in his game plan. By the time he loses patience and kicks the door in, we'll be halfway to Africa."

"Africa?"

"I didn't tell you? That's where the City is. At least, that's where the entrance is."

He took Val's hand and guided it underneath the covers, passing over his erection to the moist and avid opening beneath it.

"There's a selection of dildos in the dresser drawer. Pick one you like and fuck me, please, before we go to sleep. Afterwards, if I'm still awake, you can tell me how you came to lose your childhood."

From experience with lovers too numerous to count, Val expected Majeed to be sleeping deeply only moments after the orgasm Val wrung from him using a ridged and studded dildo of a size sufficient for pleasuring a mare. But he surprised her by remaining awake to hold and stroke her. She realized that, if Majeed insisted on considering himself as male, he was in many ways not so, the scrotal sack and penis being merely extra adornment on a body that in every other way was every bit a female's.

At first they alternated talk with lazy sensuality, remaining on a slow plateau of arousal that demanded no release but was pleasure in itself. Majeed filled a pipe with opium and smoked it as he told Val about running away from the home in England, of his days as a prostitute in Hamburg and Munich and Rome. At times Val felt uncomfortable with this confession and would interrupt the narrative with bouts of nuzzling and caressing that led to sex so indolent and languid that their lovemaking was almost tantric in its restraint. At last, with Majeed inside of her, they held each other, and Val told Majeed how she had come to be a wanderer with carnality the focus of her life.

Her introduction to the allure of the perverse, the intrigue of the wicked, had come at an early age. She had grown up in the cheerful, skylit rooms of a renovated twelve-room home on two acres of land outside Tarrant, New York. Her father, a Wall Street executive, made the ninety-minute commute to Manhattan twice a day. He had bought the showpiece home as an investment and as a haven from the tumult of city life, a safe harbor to enclose his wife and daughter while he went forth to do financial battle.

Unfortunately, his final battle, which took place when Val was five, occurred not on the Floor, but in a seedy walk-up tenement where he'd gone to do some coke with a Latina hooker. The hooker rolled him while her pimp concussed his head in several places with a tire iron. The coroner's report indicated he spent a full day dying.

Val's mother Lettie, when she learned the circumstances of the tragedy, said too bad it didn't take longer.

Apparently Anthony Petrillo had been as clever at investing and amassing money as he was unwise in the choice of his companions. He left a vast amount of money—most of which Val inherited after her mother's suicide when Val was thirteen—but little else. No memories to speak of (except the bitter ones left to his wife) and, for Val, just the blurry image of a man who left with dawn and returned long after nightfall, harried, jittery, with the look of someone deprived of sleep for so long that exhaustion comes to seem the norm and recreation aberrant in the extreme.

After her husband's death, Val's mother became afraid to leave the house. Men followed her, she claimed, when she ventured out. The idle glances and chitchat of passersby became the furtive gaze of psychopaths, the soft babbling of lunatics who stalked her. Terrorized by the demons that nested in her head, she left Val and the house to maids and cultivated a sleazy romance with agoraphobia, preening for hours before the mirror but dressing in housedresses so shabby that the maid, discovering them in a pile next to the dryer, once mistakenly used them for rags with which to polish tabletops. She spent most of her time in her sewing room, sleeping or gazing out the one window or, occasionally, stitching together a dress or blouse for Val, usually in some wildly inappropriate material: crushed velvet, lace and satin, jumpers cut from bolts of sequined silk. And all the while she muttered in no language known to any but the denizens of her own internal world, reverting to normal speech only when necessity demanded that she order groceries from the local market or fuss with local school administrators who, after a year or so, began calling repeatedly to learn why seven-year-old Val wasn't registered for school.

Almost two years after her husband's death, Lettie's weirdness took a sudden shift, one which at first appeared to be for the better. She seemed to remember Val's presence in the house and spent time with her again. Hours were spent brushing out the child's hair, caressing her, teaching her to read and write from a book of fairy tales that featured stories about seductive hags that fricasseed their children, and coiled serpents that lurked under mattresses and crawled into the snoring mouths of sleepers.

And, as if her father's murder hadn't already taught Val enough about the cruelties and caprices of the world, Lettie decided, with that obsessive single-mindedness peculiar to the insane, that more instruction for her daughter was in order.

If Lettie had been a near recluse, afraid to leave the house, now she found a black new zeal, a morbid sort of daring. She commenced to venturing out for nighttime drives into Manhattan, trolling for dissoluteness and danger like a carrion-eating bird seeking dead flesh, a madwoman and her passenger, a wide-eyed little girl.

Val remembered riding in her mother's Mercedes through the rain-soaked, late-night streets of Manhattan's seediest enclaves. Lettie always drove a brand-new car, usually one resembling a black barge, its leather smell still as fresh as when it had left the showroom. Val would sit close against her mother, staring out at the weird night-circus of the city, hoping that what she saw outside could not get in.

She remembered the sheen of stoplights reflected in oily puddles, the barred storefronts with their glut of tawdry merchandise, and the flashing neon, often with a letter or two burned out, so that the names of bars and liquor stores resembled gap-toothed grins. Often when she'd shut her eyes against the overbright display, she could still see the neon dazzle, as if one look had tattooed its garish message permanently on the inside of her eyes.

In some neighborhoods, Val remembered being most afraid when her mother stopped for lights, and the milling, seething faces passed within a few feet of the car. Blacks and whites and Orientals, all combinations in between, and, though their skins were a multitude of hues, their expressions generally were less diverse: they looked bored and angry and angry and bored, and often they looked afraid.

Sometimes Val would imagine leaping from the car and running from her mother, disappearing into the crowd's dark and perilous ranks, and throwing herself upon the mercy of their world, but she was too afraid—not only of what was inside the car with her, but of what lay outside as well.

"Lock your door," Lettie would order, but she never believed Val's confirmation that it was already securely locked. She always had to reach over and touch the lock button itself to make sure it was depressed. And all the while, her eyes would gleam, her fear and her enthrallment with that other world casting a sheen of bewitchment across her face.

"Look! Look at those two women there," Lettie would cry, pointing out two *café-au-lait* madonnas in leather skirts the size of postage stamps and wildly bouffant hair. "No, don't look yet! You don't want them to see you stare. Now, turn around now. Look!"

It was a ritual that, by the age of eight, Val already knew too well. Her mother had a name for it—"going for a ride." Presumably it was a form of education, in the wiles and sins and venalities of life, a graphic way of teaching a young child of life's rife and lurking dangers, and for a few months, Val had accepted it as such.

Only later, after she had grown too old to be trusted to remain locked inside the car on such excursions, did Val recognize the strange nocturnal forays were her mother's longing made tangible, titillation masked as moral guidance.

"See that man across the street, the one in the built-up shoes! That's a pimp, the lowest form of life. He lives off women, sells them for sex. And look there, there's his woman! That's the kind of woman that killed your father."

The hours spent cruising the tenderloin along Eighth Avenue, then over to the docks where the chickenhawks prowled like lean barracuda, and finally up into Harlem, provided a seedy circus of vicariously experienced trauma. There'd been the time a wild-eyed man, a tattooed troll with shocks of matted, grayish hair protruding at all angles from his skull, lurched up beside the car and tried to force the door open. He screamed that he was being pursued, that someone meant to kill him. Val's mother ran the light, sped off. They were halfway up the block when Val heard shots fired and saw the troll, who'd run across the street and was badgering another driver, flop facedown in a mound of dirty snow, which promptly started turning red.

At other times, men with dark faces and Halloween smiles approached the car, thinking Lettie was a well-to-do suburban matron out to score some coke. (Or better business arrangement yet, to peddle her child's ass.) They cursed her when she sped away. One time a green convertible followed them through Harlem all the way to the Triborough Bridge, its occupants an Oriental with gold stars in his teeth and a woman whose head kept disappearing and reappearing next to him like some kind of dashboard toy.

"It's so you'll see the world for what it is," Val's mother would tell her as they returned from their nocturnal jaunts. "So you'll understand how dangerous and vile men are, how careful you have to be just to survive in this world."

The source of her mother's obsession with sin and sex was never fully clear to Val, but as time went on, her mother's madness twisted inward, plunging deeper into insanity's labyrinthine maze. The late-night cruising tapered off, and here Val let her story end. She didn't tell Majeed about the night, when she was nine, that she still remembered as the night of locks and chains, the night she tried to run away and came to be a prisoner in the Sewing Room. It was the night her mother realized her beloved needles and thread were handy implements of torture and that a young girl's vagina was as dangerous as her freedom, the latter to be stolen from her, the former to be stitched shut.

To Majeed, she only said, "After Lettie stopped taking me for rides, things got much worse."

"Worse?" For a second, she thought Majeed was going to laugh and she regretted having told him anything. But he didn't laugh. He held her close. "What happened then?"

"I don't remember everything."

"That's hard to believe."

"I can remember if I want to, but it's like snipping off a piece of skin to see what shade of red the blood is. It hurts. It isn't worth it. Let's go to sleep now."

She had trained her mind to stop at this point. She knew what lay beyond and chose to go no farther. Some memories were too full of fear and grief to ever chance rekindling. Some memories required the deepest kind of burial, could only be obliterated—and then but temporarily—by pleasures of the flesh.

"Wake me, if you change your mind," Majeed said.

"No. I'll start to cry."

Majeed reached for his opium pipe and took a lazy puff. He offered it to Val. She shook her head.

"What can I do to make it better?"

Keep holding me, don't let me go, was what Val might have said.

But she needed to escape her memories, put miles and lovers between her and the past and so she said, "Just fuck me. Then take me to the City."

The trip overland to North Africa, which could have been accomplished by a few hours in the air, took Majeed and Val the better part of two weeks. Majeed suffered terribly from motion sickness. Three hours of train travel and he was invariably doubled over in the lavatory, his body sick and flowing at both ends.

Thus burdened with Majeed's unexpectedly frail stomach, they traveled in short intervals: Munich to Geneva, then south to Marseilles and Andorra, and across Spain, stopping in Granada and Seville.

In Gibraltar, they took a hydrofoil across the channel, arriving in Morocco at Tangier, then took the train south to Fez, where Majeed refused Val's offer of a few nights to relax from their journey in a luxurious hotel and booked them instead into an inexpensive hostel on the periphery of Fez, the city's once-thriving Jewish *mellah,* or neighborhood.

Val had observed that, with their arrival in North Africa, Majeed became more taciturn and moody. His consumption of opium increased dramatically, but any inquiries on Val's part as to the reason for his pique was always brushed aside; Majeed claimed he was merely fatigued or motion sick or a trick had proved disappointing.

The first night in Fez, in keeping with what was by now their pattern, they dined together, then went their separate ways, Majeed to satisfy, undoubtedly, his own proclivities, Val to explore the myriad mazelike streets of the Old City, glorying in the exotic squalor of the quarter's sights and sounds and odors. What Majeed did with his evenings was not discussed, but Val assumed he considered a night in which a few carnal transactions weren't carried out to be an evening wasted.

Rounding a corner in the Old City, Val was startled to see Majeed deep in conversation with a young Berber girl who couldn't have been more than eight or nine. Her black hair was braided intricately, her hands hennaed with jinn-spells in the custom of her tribe. The child did all the talking. Majeed listened with uncharacteristic somberness. Although she couldn't know for sure the nature of the transaction, Val's immediate assumption was less than charitable. She hadn't known Majeed cared for children; the idea that he did repulsed her. She ducked behind a passing donkey cart so that he wouldn't see her.

Usually Majeed was later coming back to whatever hotel or hostel they were lodged in, but tonight his return preceded Val's. When she entered the cramped hotel room, scarcely bigger than a walk-in closet, with its damask curtains and faded silken spread, Majeed was reclining on the bed, incense burning, the room redolent of spices and hashish. His eyes were closed, his wondrous genitalia covered with a corner of the rumpled spread. A halo of smoke drifted up from the pipe between his lips. In the dim light, his pale hair framed paler features, cascades of snow on snow.

When Val slid the chain lock into place, his eyelids lifted to pantherish slits, and he turned on her a strange, unfocused gaze.

"You're late."

"I didn't know I had a curfew."

"Don't bitch at me. I've had a shitty night. Some faggot Frenchman paid me to let him give me a blowjob in the men's room of the Hotel Palais Jamai. Then he insisted on groping me and when he found my pussy, he thought I had an extra asshole, that some disease had rotted out a hole in me." He sighed theatrically and dragged on the pipe. "He didn't get his money back, though. Fucking faggot woman-hater."

"That's quite a tale."

"Could I interest you in another one?" Majeed asked, slapping his sleek rump.

Val plopped down on the bed. "I think I'd rather hear your stories about the City. I've been patient long enough, I think."

"But we just got to Fez. We have more traveling to do."

"I thought you said Morocco was the gateway to the City," Val reminded him. "How do I even know there is such a place if you won't give me some details?"

"You trusted me this far," Majeed said. "Why not a little farther?"

"Because I'm tired of your games."

Majeed sighed heavily. "Then allow me to show you a new one."

He offered Val the pipe.

"Please, go ahead. The experience will be so much nicer for us both."

She took it, pulling the sweet, narcotic smoke into her lungs and holding it until she felt the irritation seeping out of her, replaced by a warm and scented glow that bathed her cells in languor. She took another hit. This time the smoke didn't just fill her lungs, but traveled through her bloodstream, illuminating her internal organs with what seemed to be a pale, internal glow.

She heard chimes in her voice. "What is this stuff?"

"High-quality opium."

"Quite nice."

"I think so. The only thing that's better is to have sex while you're doing it."

Val took another toke. Her head turned and she started to lie back, but the bed anticipated her direction and lifted up to meet her. Pillows, sheets, and mattress all folded round her in a soft and pliant nest.

She was wriggling into this new womb when Majeed crawled over to her and began unbuttoning her clothes.

The opium gave Majeed's body a beauty so intense that it was almost frightening. His cock, flaccid for once, was sheened like polished ivory; behind it, his labia unfurled like blossoms from some mutant flower, petals distended, redolent of musk.

He leaned forward to help Val remove her blouse. She reached up idly, ran a fingertip along his cleavage. Her gaze lingered on his face. There was something askew there, although Val was at a loss to know exactly what. The eyes, something about the eyes. That charmed-snaked look. For an instant, it had made her think of—

No! She slammed a mental door on the memory of her mother's face the night she took Val to the Sewing Room.

It's just the opium, she thought, not even wanting to guess what her own eyes must look like now. She probably had test pattern written on her pupils.

"There's plenty more where this came from," Majeed said, offering her the pipe again.

She took it, sucking first from the pipe, then on Majeed's nipple, which dangled appetizingly in her face as he leaned across her. Something cool touched Val's left wrist. She heard, as if far distant, the swish of silk.

"Now your other arm," Majeed said as he lifted away the pipe.

"What are you...?"

"I'm sure this isn't something that you're new to," said Majeed, securing Val's other wrist to the bedpost with a scarf. "But I remembered what you said about fearing confinement. Fear and arousal are so closely linked. I guessed this must be a major turn-on for you."

"It can be if..."

"I thought as much. This time will be especially memorable for you, believe me. Before we go on, would you like another hit?"

"I don't think so."

"Please. Go ahead." He put the pipe between her lips; Val drew in the fragrant smoke. "There may be parts of this that are difficult for both of us."

Majeed leaned across the bed and put his mouth to Val's. When she breathed out, he caught the smoke in his own mouth and held it.

"You don't really need to see the City," Majeed said. "I can show you many of its delights right here. Tonight."

He was rummaging around inside his suitcase. Val watched, the narcotic effect of the opium blunting her perceptions in a way she found increasingly distressing. But being bound was always a pleasure of contradictory excitements: arousal and sub-mission and panic like actors vying for center stage, each taking a turn before relinquishing the spotlight to the next. The trick, she knew from much experience, was similar to life: relax into the game, submit, and the ferocity of pleasure that resulted could be so akin to pain that the two were almost indistin-guishable.

"I've grown too fond of you for my own good," Majeed was saying.

He turned around, the effect of the narcotic in Val's system making his eyes appear more feline than ever, gold-green slits that would have bewitched her gaze entirely had she not been sud-denly distracted by the sight of what was in his hands—an eight-inch-long knife that curved up into a sweeping, saberlike blade.

"Don't worry," said Majeed. "I'm not going to use this now. I'm only going to let you look at it a while."

He ran a finger up the blade. In the pale light, it gleamed like something living, like the horn of some exotic beast lacquered with the moonlight spilling through the opening in the shades. Like Majeed's, its beauty was hypnotic. Val couldn't take her eyes off it.

"I bought it in the bazaar tonight. It's lovely, isn't it? Elegant, well-crafted, and quite cold—the way you'll soon be. When I saw it, it made me think of you."

He pressed the blade against Val's throat, nickingly close, then laid it flat atop her belly, tip pointed toward her eyes. In the warmth of the room, the steel was shockingly cold. She could feel the knobs and ridges of the heavy carved handle making tiny indentations in her flesh.

"One last thing, before I go," Majeed said. He took a pair of underpants from Val's suitcase and plugged her mouth, then secured the gag with tape. She made a sound meant to be argumentative—it came out a powerless groan reminiscent of Santos's inhuman sounds.

"I doubt that you'd cry out, but one can't take the chance. Especially when I tell you I'm going to kill you. Few believe me when I tell them that at this point, but you might be the exception. I can't take that chance."

He bent down and closed Val's eyelids, kissed them both, then unlocked the door, admitting for an instant only a few words of an argument shouted out in Arabic up the hall, the aroma of couscous and lamb simmering somewhere nearby, then he was gone. She lay there, staring at the knife blade lit up with moon. Her skin tingled at its proximity. Her fingers ached to touch its metal blade.

It was a game, of course, a brutal game meant to seduce with terror. She reassured herself of this so many times it started to sound true, until Majeed's fundamental harmlessness seemed as inexorable as the law of gravity.

She tried to work the scarves up over the bedposts, though—just in case—but found them snagged beneath some baroque convexity of the post's design, impossible to slide. Sleep seemed unthinkable, and yet she dozed, dabbling first at the edges of unconsciousness like one wading in the shallows of deep water before plunging, unexpectedly and with mounting fright, into dreams that rushed at her in fragments, like jagged glass. Nightmares flashing past in jigsaw form held to no particular pattern except the terror they inspired.

"Do you like to bleed?"

She thought at first it was another nightmare, this one masking its counterfeit nature behind a facsimile of Majeed's voice. Then the pain bit into her, and she came awake with a muffled gasp. Majeed stood by the bed, the knife in hand. The cool blade gleamed with blood. She looked down, saw the shallowest of incisions extending in a line between pubic hair and navel. In places, the skin wasn't even broken. In others, her blood bubbled up like scarlet sweat.

She tried to speak. The gag reduced her words to the gurgling of an imbecile or choking victim. Majeed wiped the blood off on her flank. He caressed the blade across her throat. The lightest of pressures, barely enough to dent the skin.

"I could slash your trachea and you'd never speak again."

He moved the blade up to one of her bound wrists. "Or open up the veins here and let you bleed to death."

He traced the blade across Val's face, lingering on her eyelids, her nose. "Or I could simply remove the parts of your face that make you look human. You'd be surprised how long you could live in that condition. Assuming that you'd want to."

She made a helpless, rasping sound. Her eyes followed his every twitch, beseeching leniency. If this was a game, the point of pleasure was long past. Her wrists ached. Her heart stuttered with terror, its every beat seeming to squeeze out more drops of blood from the cuts across her belly. Majeed held the knife vertically between her eyes, so close she couldn't focus on it properly. She saw only Majeed's pallid face, insectile in its out-of-focusness, bisected by the glimmering slash of silver.

Then a deft flicking of Majeed's wrist and sudden pain— blood clung in ruby droplets from her left earlobe before dripping off to plunk hotly upon her shoulder. Val thrashed upon the bed, eyes darting from the knifepoint to Majeed's eyes and back again and back....

She couldn't get Majeed to meet her eyes. That, more than anything he'd yet done, terrified her. He teased her with the knife a while, not cutting her again, but running the blade across her flesh like a divining rod. When Majeed laid down the knife again, he finally met her eyes, but Val's hopes faltered: There was neither ice nor heat in them, only distance, as though he looked at her from some schizoid universe where pain and love were meaningless in equal measure.

"Since you don't seem to be enjoying this, I might as well."

He began withdrawing objects from his pants pockets. Hypodermic syringe and powder: the talismans of addiction. Soon he was busy with the paraphernalia of his habit. He tipped a bit of heroin from bag to spoon, then cooked it with a cigarette lighter held underneath. All this Val watched with stricken eyes, imploring him to end the game but failing to find the least compassion in his vacant gaze. When it came time to tie his arm off and shoot up, Majeed turned his attention back to Val.

"Understand that I don't want to do this. But if you scream, I'll cut your vocal cords. So consider very carefully before you yell for help."

So saying, he reached behind Val's head and freed her mouth, then used the scarf to tie off a vein.

"Majeed, if this is a game…"

"It's not a game. It's what I have to do."

"What does that mean?"

"It means I owe somebody."

"Filakis, isn't it?"

"Yes."

"You owe him…?"

"A life, taken in a bloody fashion."

"Why mine?"

"Your curiosity has a self-destructive bent. It led you to search for the City. It also led you to me, the one who's going to kill you."

"Why *my* life, Majeed?"

"Because he enjoys suffering and he knows I…" he grimaced,

searching for the vein. "Look, just shut up or I'll find something else to gag you with."

"Don't do this. Please. I can't die yet."

He tilted a derisive eyebrow and concentrated on drawing the heroin up into the syringe.

"It's not as though most people expect to choose the moment. Besides, you told me you preferred dangerous...people. This was bound to happen sooner or later. Your lifestyle almost demands an untimely end, wouldn't you agree?"

"But not like this...not you."

"I'm as competent a killer as the next."

"At least...you said you'd take me to the City. Do that at least and then..."

"Shut up! You don't know what you're asking for. There's no such place. It's a lie, a myth, dreamed up by people bored by everything else life has to offer, bored out of their minds, quite literally."

"Don't make me die like this. Not shackled like the way..."

"...the way someone once did to you? Who was it, Val? The friendly old physician, the priest? A funny uncle or your crazy mother? What did she *do* to you?"

"What do you...?"

"No, never mind. It's too late now. Besides I'm tired of listening to you prattle. When I'm not using you for sex, you're really very tiresome."

The syringe was full. Majeed squirted out a tiny bit to clear air bubbles. He struck at the vein and missed. His hands trembled so violently the needle appeared to dance.

"Majeed, what did you mean before? About why Filakis wants me to be the one you kill?"

"Shut up. It doesn't matter. I promised him I would or he won't let me back into..."

"The City? Isn't that it? So that's who Filakis really is, the Turk."

"What difference does it make?"

"Is the place that wonderful? That you'd kill me if Filakis said it was the only way you'd get back in? If that's the case, why did you ever leave? Why didn't you just stay there?"

Majeed's inability to hit a vein was making him increasingly distraught. Sweat beaded on his forehead, ran down his face.

"Is it like the opium?" Val pressed. "You want to stop, you want to leave, but you can't? It always pulls you back, and you pay any price for readmittance?"

"Shut up!" shouted Majeed and threw the syringe aside.

Val held her breath. The effect of the opium had diminished beneath the more potent effect of terror, and if she was still high, she couldn't tell it. She felt petrified, frozen in her fear like an insect trapped in amber, her muscles tense as wires, her heart unbeating stone.

If I'm going to die, she thought, *let it be something memorable.*

Majeed picked up the knife and came over to the bed. He traced the dark line of dried blood that bisected Val's belly, then lifted the blade tip to her neck. It popped the skin an inch above the hollow at her throat and pooled there before over-spilling and streaming down her ribs. The pain was distant, unremarkable, her senses pinpointed entirely on Majeed.

"Why am I the one you have to kill?" she whispered. "Why not someone else?"

"Goddamn you."

"Why me?"

Majeed raised the knife. His voice was barely audible, the low whistle of insect wings. "Because he knows I love you, damn you."

He raised the knife and brought it down—twice in quick succession. The blade slashed flesh, but only superficially. The main direction of the thrust was through the scarves that bound Val's arms.

Majeed waved a dismissive hand. "Go on and live your wretched life. You'll end up murdered anyway. It just won't be by me."

Val breathed again. She rolled off the bed, struggling into items of her clothing with arms that had gone numb as logs, no longer under her command but senseless stobs of flesh. She beat the circulation back into them, had managed to put on a pair of jeans when Majeed suddenly leaped across the bed and stood before her, bloody knife in hand. His eyes were wild, his skin an unnatural, sickly cast, malarial.

"Wait!"

She thought he'd changed his mind about sparing her life.

"Please, Majeed, let's…"

His knife hand began to tremble. Val lunged past him for the door. Majeed grabbed her arm and flung her backward onto the bed.

"I said you can't…"

But Val heard it now, the footsteps approaching up the hall. She had no reason to think they heralded disaster except from Majeed's reaction, which left little doubt as to his terror. He was darting about the room in a frantic dance of wasted motion, a trapped gerbil, running from window to window in a hopeless effort to find some avenue of escape.

"No," said Val, when it became clear Majeed meant to jump. "It's too high. You'll kill yourself."

Their room was three floors up. Both windows overlooked a narrow, stone-paved alleyway crowded not only with passersby but with a hodgepodge of vendors, their wares spread out on mats upon the stones. A fall from this height, though possibly not fatal, would shatter bones and organs.

Still, Majeed was forcing one of the windows up and would clearly have taken his chances with the fall had not the door, which Majeed had locked upon his return to the room, suddenly burst inward.

The Turk, in all his corrupt nobility, strode across to the window and locked an arm that was all vein and sinew around Majeed's throat.

"You betrayed me, bitch," he crooned in Majeed's ear. "You promised me her life tonight. You swore."

Majeed responded by twisting with reptilian grace, the knife still in his hand. Filakis wrenched it from Majeed's grip and hurled it across the floor. Val heard fingerbones and joints crunch sickeningly. Majeed wailed.

"Don't," said Filakis, guessing Val's intention toward the knife.

He twisted Majeed around, so he could face Val. Behind him

the open door tempted with the possibility of escape, but Filakis barred the way. He stared at Val—an odd and terrifying sizing up of her that seemed rife with disgust, abhorrence.

Meanwhile, Majeed struggled in his captor's arms, choking and sputtering as Filakis applied more pressure to his neck. There was something odd about Filakis's palms, Val noted. At first, she'd had the impression that they were smeared with blood. Then, she realized the man's flesh was hennaed with jinn-spells and incantations, a practice designed to ward off evil spirits that she'd observed among the Berber women.

But Val had little time to reflect upon the oddity of the Turk's indulgence in this superstition. The knife he'd wrested from Majeed lay within easy reach, a temptation that, in the present circumstances, was irresistible. Val grabbed it, thinking to plant the blade in Filakis's bony neck and would have done so, had she not been halted by a crackling sound and the unfolding of a spectacle before her that rendered her immobile.

Tongues of pale green fire were licking at Filakis and Majeed. Mere tatters, at first, the flames soon grew, tonguing and plucking at Majeed's face and breasts, at his captor's opulence of hair. Majeed writhed and screamed in Filakis's grasp, but the Turk uttered not one cry as the fire climbed his torso, igniting flesh and clothing in its luminous embrace.

Majeed stretched out a hand to Val.

She reached to take it, but fire blossomed from her lover's fingertips like thorns. There was a moment's indecision, when Val might have grabbed Majeed's hand anyway, but the flames were devouring with such speed that, in the instant that she hesitated, Majeed's hand was burned away, the fingers curling back upon themselves like desiccated fetuses.

Electric, crackling tendrils spread across Majeed's and Filakis's faces. Skin cracked and peeled. What lay below, shimmering suet and tendon and bone, was soon unveiled and melted down. All cries stopped and, presently, all motion.

The flame bulged out at its height and formed a funnel, which whirled like some inhuman dervish about the floor, consuming what remained. For several seconds, it danced and capered on the carpet with terrible exuberance, then lost volume and momentum and sputtered out into a tiny heap of rubble and cold ash upon the floor.

Left behind, for an instant only, there glowed an afterimage: steepled towers and squat, dun-colored houses, shimmering like bleak mirages behind medieval walls. The walls, when Val peered closer, appeared to be composed of writhing human bodies, living, faceless, and crudely formed, all locked in carnal congress.

Val blinked—the scene did not disperse, but took on form, dimension. There was a moment when, remembering it later, she was sure she could have simply walked inside the rent in space that appeared open to her. But by the time she gathered wits and courage, the image turned translucent, its third dimension sloughing off like worn-out skin, the remaining threads of form and color liquefying into a few drops of dewlike mist that hovered in the air, then dispersed to nothing.

Even as the shock of seeing Majeed's fate rooted her in place, a small burst of celebration fired her heart. The place she'd glimpsed could be nowhere except the City. That, or Hell, and she meant to find out, one way or another.

Majeed and his mysterious abductor had left behind a small pile of remnants on the floor. She went over to inspect it. Swatches of cloth and leather, scorched and frayed as though they'd been through an incinerator, Majeed's opium pipe, or what was left of it, reduced to a lump of ivory and melted gold, dollops of glass, coin-sized, that must have once been a hypodermic syringe.

And something else: a pale green piece of stone, slightly smaller than a hen's egg, rounded at the top but with a flat base. Val picked it up and turned it over in her hand. The object was similar to a number of the incense burners Majeed had set out on the windowsill—in the case of the latter, the top could be unscrewed and removed to reveal the candle contained inside.

Unlike the incense burners, however, this jar offered no seam to indicate where the top could be twisted off. It seemed to be a solid piece of stone, onyx or malachite perhaps. If so, its function was entirely ornamental, yet so closely did it resemble the others that Val couldn't help but think a seam existed somewhere in its intricately carved sides, but was simply far more subtly crafted and inconspicuously designed.

She turned the small jar in her hands a dozen times, yet found nothing to indicate it opened into halves. Its varnished surface was carved with some kind of complex floral pattern. Leafy spirals and overlapping whorls interlocked in patterns that at first appeared both random and simple, but, upon closer inspection, proved to be teasingly complex, provocative in their design. Stamenlike shafts writhed and twisted into budded knots upon the top while along the sides, carved blossoms formed fantastic arabesques that defeated each attempt Val made to trace them to their source in the design.

At length she put the object down, but not before it had revealed at least one secret. At the warmth of her hands, it began to emit the faintest of odors, a musk so subtle in its fragrance that Val could sense it only with her nose pressed to the stone.

In any case, there was no time for further inspection. In the courtyard down below, a crowd had formed among the vending stalls, people gazing up at the room where someone must have seen the flickering of flames. Val heard shouted Arabic and French. At this hour, the hostelry was locked up for the night, but men were rattling at the gate, yelling undoubtedly for the proprietor to come down and unlock the door.

Val had no wish to be caught and questioned. She grabbed her tote bag with passport and wallet and headed through the shattered door toward the back stairwell. The carved piece of stone she slipped inside her pocket with a promise to herself that it would yield its secrets to her yet.

For a few more days, Val remained in Fez in the hope that Majeed might somehow still be alive and make his way back to her, but restlessness soon overcame her. She took the train southwest to Marrakesh, then to the beach resort of Agadir. From there, she traveled to the town of Taroudant, a market center tucked in a valley between the High Atlas and Anti-Atlas Mountains. Always she kept the incense burner in her pocket, to be brought out and handled at odd moments, its complexities explored.

In Taroudant, whose marketplace offered natural toiletries made from the musk of gazelle glands and desiccated lizards sold as potions to ensure good health, Val spent hours studying the carved convolutions. It seemed to her that, over time, a pattern could be discerned and that occasionally, upon repeating a particular sequence of touch, the scent emanating from the jar became more powerful. At times, the scent was so alluring that she focused only on the jar, blind to the sights and sounds around her as she gave in to her obsession.

It was toward the end of her fourth day in Taroudant, while taking refuge from the high heat of early afternoon in her hotel room, that Val first felt the minuscule beginning of a dismantling of the jar's design. A portion of its pattern seemed suddenly to be less than solidly attached. Val shut her eyes and traced the complex arabesques like Braille. There was a subtle sliding, followed by a snap, and an odor almost indecent in its seductiveness wafted to her nostrils. She looked down in her palm and saw a tiny aperture had opened up in the center of one carved whorl. A half-inch wick, the kind found on any ordinary candle, protruded up.

Before she lost her courage, Val lit a match and touched it to the wick. A flame like a serpent tongue swayed forth. Val took a step backward; the flame grew and leaned in her direction, as though sniffing her out. It split into two tongues, which forked again until the greater portion of the wall was covered with a tree of emerald fire. The tree limbs undulated, spread, and Val could see that within each searing branch and twig were silhouetted spectral couplings: a compendium of every sort of depravity, every sexual excess of which flesh is capable.

Val stared into the flame, felt its obscene allure.

"Majeed," she said and touched her hand to it.

A hand was all the flame required. A fingernail, she realized later, would have sufficed. The fire seized her, fed. There was no burning, but a cold and weightless dazzle and then a light that blinded, deafened, numbed, with her senses being subtracted until all that remained was the odor of desire, and that odor suffused every pore and everywhere it brought oblivion.

It was the wind that woke her. It was full of sand and stinging hot, and yet each particle of sand that blew against her skin was like a tiny, tingling penetration, invigorating and indecent.

She got to her feet, felt eyes on her. A bearded Bedouin was staring at her from behind a donkey's dappled flanks. Man and beast made not a sound, but a slow and almost imperceptible thrusting on the man's part, a look of stoic boredom on the donkey's countenance, told her the nature of the mute transaction. Such acts weren't to Val's taste, and yet she had to force herself to look away. The sand was nipping at her flesh like lovers' kisses, the wind hotly seductive as it whirled through her hair.

At first glance at her surroundings, it appeared to Val that she was still inside the city of Taroudant, looking up at its pale pink, crenelated walls, its decaying medieval ramparts. Yet it was different. But for the bearded sodomite with his equine mate and a few haggard old people, the streets seemed strangely empty. Only the evidence of commerce—huge burlap bags of grain, their contents in big golden piles upon the ground, bright yellow *babouches,* or slippers, tapestries, and vegetables—argued for some semblance of normal city life.

From somewhere in the winding, shadowed streets, a chime echoed. Its silvery tones shivered through Val's body; its vibrations pleasured heart and lungs and entrails. The sound came again, melodic, light. Val leaned against a wall, flustered by her body's unequivocal response to the sound. A parrot flew by above—a gaudy slash of green and scarlet against searing blue sky—and the sight brought delight that was almost unbearable in its intensity. Nor were simple, everyday sensations less capable of inspiring ecstasy. The odor of bread baking, of overripe persimmons and citrus smells and almonds, of musky human sweat that wafted from the cloistered doorways as she passed— each was author to an exquisite sensitivity of mind and loins, making of each pore a tiny vulva, ravenous for more.

She wandered the mazelike streets and tunneled corridors, aware of others who observed her, their eyes taking her in like the languid scent of some new flower as she passed before them, this newcomer to their center, but staying always out of her sight. Occasionally, in the rapid turning of a corner, the sudden glance behind her back, Val was positive she glimpsed some of the City's inhabitants. It was difficult, if not impossible, however, to keep her concentration focused—when the slap of her sandaled feet on paving stones, the metallic ting of chimes, the gold threads in an ornately woven rug glimpsed in an open courtyard wrung such sensual delight that she felt exhausted, frazzled, giddy with the unnatural opulence of her surroundings.

As her wanderings led her deeper into the labyrinthine streets, Val caught sight, here and there, of other people: an old woman lying splay-legged in an alleyway, her grizzled, thinly furred sex exposed. She held a musical instrument, a long flute-like thing with a curved end, which she simultaneously used to play and penetrate herself, moaning out the notes as she played herself to orgasm.

At another intersection, the narrowness of the convergence forced Val to step around a copulating trio, two men and a young woman locked in silent rut, one penetrating the woman's cunt, the other buggering her in an almost somnambulistic torpor. They barely moved as Val passed by, but the sex-scent wafting off them was enough to make her reel, her vaginal muscles clenching and releasing with contractions.

Still farther on, a narrow passageway opened up into a courtyard where two naked women embraced within the rippling shallows of a fountain, one sucking on the other's breasts while the first leaned back and spread her legs, the better to allow the cascade of water access to her clitoris. And there was the goateed man she passed who grunted and sighed out ecstacies as he made love to an ornately painted gourd, an aperture carved out of its pulpy meat to allow for such conveniences. He took no note of Val's presence, but bucked and thrust arhythmically, the gourd's surface already slicked with evidence of previous man-vegetable love.

A dozen or so yards on, Val came upon a square devoted to magicians, storytellers, and oddities of every sort: Here a tattooed boy made fire caper up and down his arms, then masturbated with the flames. A nude woman whose only covering was the strawberries and lemons sewn into her skin did a slow, lewd dance. A dark-skinned man picked dates and olives off the ground with a prehensile penis; another bent his ten-inch cock backward and belabored his own anus.

In the midst of such monstrosities, a Berber girl with eyes like sapphires and emeralds held up her brightly hennaed hands so Val could see the spells tattooed there. She caught Val's eye. Her hands wove mysteries. In the space of several eyeblinks, she transformed herself into a goat, an aging hag, a priapic dwarf. Val stared, trying to get at the root of the illusion, but her eyes were always drawn back to the tattoos on the child's palms, where the illusions seemed to be created by some hypnotic effect induced by the movements of her illustrated hands.

At length, she forced herself along, although exhaustion was leeching at her enthusiasm for further exploration. Indeed, all the people she encountered seemed depleted, slacked. Even those who copulated with each other did so not with the natural frenziedness of lust, but in a kind of stupor, like lewd sleepwalkers who, upon colliding with each other in a darkened hall, engage in mating more from habit than desire and without ever being aroused sufficiently to waken fully.

As the afternoon wore on toward dusk, she became aware of moving shadows, skeletal denizens of the City creeping out to find each other, meeting and merging with scarcely so much as a cry before interlocking lips and loins. Yet even then there was less a sense of passion than of a famished mutual feeding upon each other. Sometimes the wraith-lovers interrupted their mating to follow Val a pace or two, but they were slow and clumsy, their unsavory caresses easy to elude. More than once, she gingerly intruded on an embrace to ask about Majeed, but the inhabitants of the City seemed to understand no language but the one of touch and offered her no answers but their own slicked cocks and cum-soaked thighs and parted, pungent vulvas.

The streets grew steeper, narrower. She peered inside a courtyard and discovered a tannery where animal skins were soaked in stinking vats before being transferred to a row of dark, dank rooms. Here silent figures pulled the fur with ghoulish zeal, then stretched and beat the skin while others took the opportunity to yank their own hard meat, so that the smell of cum commingled with that of the tanning juices. The very repugnance of the place was sickeningly seductive. Val didn't linger long.

A short way beyond the reeking tanneries, she came upon a marketplace little different in outer appearance from those she had encountered in Moroccan cities of a more conventional nature. Only the wares displayed were a departure from the usual—on one blanket, a treasury of dildos in every size and shape, on the next, a sadist's spree of whips and clamps and restraints, across the way a man who sprawled supine, mouth plugged with a gigantic dildo which he offered up, beckoning to passersby to sit upon his face and take their pleasure there. He didn't lack for business; a line had formed and both sexes took their turn lowering themselves upon his phallus-mouth.

A few blocks beyond the souks, Val was almost sideswiped by a nude and legless man, a repulsive lummox propelling himself along on gorilla-muscled arms, penis swelling up obscenely to bob against a convex bud of navel. He was obese and hideously mutilated, his chest and shoulders stitched with scars as though some mad graffiti artist had used his flesh for scrawling.

Val felt a deep, internal shiver. Dismayed by her reaction, she tried to look away but the man was staring at her with a gaze of open invitation. His strangely luminous eyes compelled respect, each blink a blatant proposition that weakened her with want. Appalled by her own desire, she approached the vulgar wretch and squatted over him. She took in all his ugliness, the cock in full and virile jut between the stumps, the corded arms, the scabbed and scarified chest. Obscene he was—and bloated, gross—and yet his very repugnance increased her lust.

He urged her on in Arabic. She spread her legs and lowered herself, letting her skirt flare out as she set her weight, impaled herself. The lemon-emerald eyes half closed. He sighed and thrust. She reached back and clutched his stumps. The scars were odd, not flat or smooth but intricately textured, whorled, and ridged. The motif was familiar now; it brought to mind the ridged stone of the incense burner, of doorways wildly arabesqued, of hennaed hands, of...

"You!"

She pulled back, even as the man impaling her began a seamless transformation: Broad hirsute chest reshaping into nubile breasts, slabbed cheekbones and simian forehead refining into the almond eyes and heart-shaped face of the Berber child-magician. At the appalled look on Val's face, the little girl pealed forth bright laughter. She held up those gorgeous, hennaed hands so that—for an instant only—Val could stare transfixed at the lurid dazzle of the moving patterns on her palms.

The child leaned forward, touched her lips to Val's. Her kiss seared.

Val let her lips part. The Berber girl's tongue tasted of mint and honey.

"Majeed?" the girl asked. "You want?"

Val nodded and replied in French, "Where is he?"

Like the keeper of some wondrous secret, the child smiled slyly. She led Val through more winding streets to a stone stairway that descended between red mud walls. After the first few steps, the darkness was impenetrable, the air tainted with a sewer stench that made Val's stomach roil.

They reached a landing, where the Berber girl produced a flashlight from her trouser pocket and proceeded down yet another, steeper flight of stairs. She moved with such sureness and fluidity that Val had to struggle to keep up. Occasionally she paused to catch her breath and heard, emerging from below, the most distressing sounds, plaintive wails and frenzied keening, the staccato yap of tongues convulsed by insanity or pain.

At the deepest point of their descent, they stood before a bleak and narrow corridor of ancient prison cells. *A dungeon,* thought Val. The girl pointed ahead and indicated Val should proceed, that she'd come as far as she intended to go. Val hesitated.

"Majeed!" the child said, scowling.

Val peered into the gloom. "I can't."

The girl relinquished her light to Val and motioned for her to continue, repeating Majeed's name. The noise level, at the entrance to the corridor, had by this time intensified to a din. Sounds of suffering and, perhaps more disturbingly, low moans and sighs that either pain or passion might be father to. Holding the light ahead of her, Val continued on her own.

A few paces farther on, the narrowing staircase petered out entirely at a hole in the wall where a stone had been removed. It was from the other side that the sounds of suffering were emanating. Val crouched, holding her candle out before her, and slithered through the opening.

She found herself in another corridor, this one even grimmer than the one she'd just traversed. On either side were narrow cells, each one containing an isolated occupant. Ripe with youth or withered with age, the effeminate and virile, the bestial and the lovely, each endured his or her own ordeal—some hooded, with clamps attached to swollen genitals and nipples, others forced to sit upon huge dildos that stretched anuses and vaginas to the ripping point. Still others suffered cock rings of heated metal and brutally snug corsets, bindings so unnaturally tight the flesh popped between the ropes like risen bread. One man, a contortionist, was positioned on his back with legs behind his head. His cock came within a millimeter of his mouth but so cunningly was he secured that not even his most ardent struggling allowed his tongue to reach his engorged head.

Val wandered on, appalled and mesmerized by this symphony of frustrated arousal. The floor became increasingly wet. She heard a soft sloshing and, rounding a bend in the torturous hallway, saw a shallow pool just large enough to accommodate a body. In it, nude and bound, leeched utterly of color, floated face down an emaciated angel, dead to all appearances but with a breathing tube resembling a small flute extending from its mouth. Given its pallor and stillness, Val was highly doubtful the thing was capable of breath at all.

She ran the flashlight beam along the creature's body and gasped with recognition. No ethereal being this, but quite the opposite—Majeed. But in what condition! Fetuslike, he floated in his swollen sac of womb. Naked, touching nothing, ensconced in darkness and silence.

Val reached into the pool and floated Majeed over toward her until she could untie his hands and flip him on his back. Dead, she thought. Pale and, to all appearances, devoid of life, his clammy flesh seemed formed from tallow and slimed with ashen mucus. Yet Val had already witnessed sufficient wonders in the place not to concede Majeed's lifelessness too soon.

She lifted Majeed's head out of the pool, removed the tube from his mouth and shook him hard. His head lolled back and forth, his eyewhites gleamed. He didn't seem to breath, but, with a hand between his breasts, Val felt the ticking of his heart, its pace so slow that her own heart beat a dozen times to Majeed's one.

"Majeed!"

She slapped his head from side to side, then bit him on the ear until blood flowed. His eyes came slowly into focus, squinting into the painful glare of the flashlight. His skin and hair, always fair, were alabaster. He looked, Val thought, like an albino eel raised in some subterranean cavern, its translucent flesh never touched by sunlight.

"Majeed, it's Val. What have they done to you?"

Majeed began to shake and then to sob. With Val's help, he managed to drag himself up over the side of the pool where he collapsed shivering, his nerves capering in mad jigs beneath the skin, tics working at his face and muscle twitches making his limbs flail.

Val realized then the nature of his peculiar torture. In a world where even the rustling of leaves produced erotic shivers, Majeed had been deprived of even the most meager stimulation—even his beloved opium had been denied him.

Val's hands were covered with the liquid from the pool. She became aware now of the coolness and viscosity of what at first she'd taken to be water. Not water, though, she realized now, but cold and clotted semen.

"Majeed? Answer me. Come on, get up."

She hoisted Majeed to a sitting position and struck him in the back. He took a gasping breath of air, then another. His eyelids fluttered open and he gazed at her, as mindless as an idiot child before leaning over and vomiting into the pool.

"How did you...?"

"It doesn't matter," Val said. "Right now, we've got to hurry and get out."

She led Majeed back along the corridor with its rows of cells and naked captives, through the opening in the wall where she had first gained access. Far ahead, a wan light filtered down.

"Who put you there?" Val said.

"Filakis, of course."

"But why?"

"To punish me for not killing you that night in Fez. But mostly to amuse himself. He's not like the others here…he can't enjoy real pleasure. He has to get it watching others or torturing them."

They'd reached the lower landing of the staircase. Majeed suddenly stopped and grabbed Val's hand.

"Wait. I need…it's been so long without…"

"Your drugs, you mean?"

"My drug of choice," Majeed said. He grabbed Val's hand and pressed her fingers to his groin. His penis felt achingly erect, his vulva dripping juices. Something new had been added to Majeed's anatomy since his captivity, a set of gold rings penetrated labia and scrotum, made a bell-like tinging as he maneuvered Val against the wall and tried to lift her skirt.

"There isn't time!"

But terror, as Val had long known, was the most potent of aphrodisiacs, and sex within the City's walls was sex magnified a hundredfold, each orgasm an intoxicant that bewitched the mind for days. Majeed's hunger called to hers, and soon her legs were open, allowing him to rut his fill.

"Turn around."

She braced herself against the stones and shut her eyes. Majeed thrust inside her, his motion making the vulval rings clink and ping together. He gave a moan that Val thought to be his climax. But there came an instant when he lost contact with her entirely, when her inner muscles clenched on emptiness, and Majeed's vulval bells were stilled too suddenly.

"Majeed?"

She tried to turn around, but her wrists were clasped and manacled behind her. From the corner of her vision, Val saw Majeed slump to the floor. Behind her, she smelled an unspeakable aroma, a perfumed breath, rich with death and strawberries.

She managed to twist around. Filakis stood before her, lean and dour as a medieval saint. His hennaed fingers, long, El Grecoesque, roved her face as though its contours held the meaning of some mystery. His lips, drawn tight in monkish gloom, bestowed a cold kiss on her forehead, but Val's attention was distracted by his nudity and by a nakedness far worse, the almost total absence of any genitalia. His testicles were absent altogether; his penis, what remained of it, had been reduced to a limp and useless teat.

He noted the direction of her gaze and smiled almost apologetically. "Ah, I see you've noticed my...deformity. Well, let me say, I wasn't born like this. It was my choice. A eunuch savors pleasure vicariously, you see, and I'm particularly skilled at that. It pleases me to think that, while others soil themselves in a thousand nauseating ways, I stay untouched. Pure, if you will. My pleasure comes from taking sex in any form except my own. Let others wallow in dung, their filth never touches me."

"I only came to get Majeed," Val said. "You've punished him enough. Now let us leave."

"Majeed? Oh, you mean *her*," said Filakis. "The creature pretends to be a male, but she's a cunt and nothing else."

"More reason not to need her then."

Filakis smiled. "Your haste to leave verges on insulting. I thought you wanted pleasure. That's why you went to so much trouble coming here. I can't let you go away disappointed." He smiled. "But maybe I was wrong. Maybe you're like so many others and what you secretly desire and pine for is what you most deeply dread."

He touched Val's throat while keeping hold on her manacled hands. The long, emaciated fingers closed and gripped, wringing forth a rain of gold and silver coins behind her eyes. The coins clattered against the inside of her skull, but then the din grew distant, faint, was replaced at length by one exquisite, terrifying orgasm...then nothingness.

Val's body, when she first opened her eyes, was reflected back to her in the ceiling's mirrored tiles. Her physical condition alarmed and sickened her. Every inch of her, from collarbones to pubis, upper arms to wrists, appeared to be the canvas on which a demented seamstress had created a masterpiece of color and design. A hundred needles pierced Val's flesh, and through the punctures had been woven the most colorful of threads, which crisscrossed in a splendid zigzag of geometry. The threads, in turn, were tied to hooks nailed into the bed's headboard and sides. Her slightest movement, therefore, even a breath drawn in too sharply, caused the needles to plunge deeper beneath the skin and her nerves to scream out in ungodly unison.

Movement created pain so sharp and constant that, after a time, it crossed a psychic border and became a kind of lunatic arousal. In this, Val realized, lay the peculiar horror of the City, its ability to wring appetite from even the most appalling cruelties, the most demeaning humiliations. Desire not linked to satisfaction in the slightest way, but a perverse and masochistic lust that fed on misery as fervently as those in the outside world generally sought comfort.

She learned all this in her strange and all too familiar prison, a room she had only to glimpse for one brief second to know its parameters and furnishings, the contents of its bookshelves and its dresser drawers, to know, without going near the window, what view she would see: not crenelated walls of a Moroccan Casbah, but plowed fields and distant tree-clad hills, a decaying barn belonging to some unknown neighbors to the east and a silo above whose entranceway a hex sign had been drawn. To know that if she were free to turn the photo on the desktop to face her, she would see a picture of the person she had been, the child who was held prisoner in the Sewing Room.

How such an illusion of a return to the chamber of her childhood captivity was possible was lost on Val. She assumed, at first, some sort of hallucination was at work, that Filakis had, unknown to her, slipped some type of drug into her system. This belief was comforting for it implied that, at some point, the drug might either wear off or be overcome by sheer force of will, and she resolved not to give in to panic but to simply accept her fate for the moment and await the next development the way one allows a nightmare to run its course in the confidence of, at some point, awakening.

When she heard a key turn in the lock, Val prayed to see Filakis even as a part of her mind braced for something worse. It came. What entered the room wasn't Filakis but her mother Lettie or something identical to her right down to the dimple in her left cheek, the small scar above one eyebrow.

"How are we, sweetheart?" crooned the Lettie creature, mincing across the room with a breakfast-laden tray. Val didn't have to look to know the contents: toast and milk, half a grape-fruit, a jar of honey.

"How do we feel now? Better?"

"These stitches...whatever they are...they hurt."

"Well...naturally..." said Lettie, no more moved by Val's predicament than she'd been twenty-five years earlier. "That's so you won't get up and leave. But the laces are quite beautiful, I think." She set the tray down on the desk and strummed a lac-quered fingernail idly across the weave. Like falling dominos, Val's nerves responded to the wiggling needles. Fire shot beneath her skin. She howled.

"...This design in particular I find attractive. A cat's cradle, don't you see? Much prettier than any clothing you could wear."

The pain receded. Val tried to concentrate on the apparition at her side. She was as Val remembered her, plump and auburn-haired and artfully made up. False eyelashes and rouge and Cleopatra lids, a Vegas showgirl gone to seed but handsome still and not a day older than when Val had been her pet and pris-oner in the upstairs room in Tarrant.

"Please..."

Lettie made a shushing sound and leaned over Val. Her mouth was crammed with needles that protruded from it like sil-ver fangs. One by one, she threaded them, replaced them in her mouth. Pinching up a bit of flesh from the underside of Val's breast she ran the needle through. Val gasped with pain and fright, but she dared not struggle too much for the least move-ment on her part caused the other needles to shift and dig.

"This is going to be so beautiful."

"Please stop. Please let me up."

"But then you might run away. The world is such a danger-ous place. You might hurt yourself."

The words were spoken with the correct tone, the perfect inflection that the real Lettie, were she living, would have used. Val blinked and tried to clear the apparition from her mind. "You're dead," Val said. "You killed yourself after someone saw me at the window and called the police, and they took me away from you."

"Hush now. All that was only a bad dream. It's over now. Come here now and look out the window."

"I can't move. You can see that, can't you?"

Lettie sighed. "No, I suppose not. Then I'll bring the view to you."

The window didn't budge, but Val's mind suddenly filled with long-forgotten images. The winding dun-colored streets of the City disappeared, and it was spring in upstate New York, and the earth smelled fresh and thawed. Green buds were visible on the trees, and swallows, so far away they looked like asterisks in full flight against the sky, did airborne lifts and plummets. On the road beyond the untilled land, a man was passing by on horseback. He wore a cowboy hat and his boots must have been tipped with metal, for now and then the sun would catch just the right angle and a blinding shaft, a pin of light, would blaze and spangle. He moved farther and farther out of sight, until his horse and he were no bigger than the swallows, a pinpoint of light, a disappearing diamond. He was, thought Val, the most beautiful thing she'd ever seen and as unattainable as the most distant star.

Tears filled Val's eyes. She knew the scene was an illusion, produced perhaps by Filakis's trickery or her own weary, traumatized mind, but the needles in her flesh were real. With the slightest hint of movement, the arabesque of threads across her body tightened and a hundred tiny wounds were enlarged and deepened.

"Don't you like to look?" said Lettie.

"Of course."

"Then why are you crying?"

Val tried to turn her head to indicate her bonds, but even this small effort was rewarded with myriad needle stings, sweet silver bees that set upon her at the faintest shiver.

"It's painful to look out there and see the world and not be able to be in it."

"I know *I* wouldn't want to be out there," said Lettie, and she wiggled one of the needles just under Val's left arm.

"Why not?" said Val, awash in pain.

"The dangers."

"But think," Val said, "of the possibilities for pleasure."

"No!" Lettie's face contorted viciously. She made a choking, half-mad sound, and stomped her feet so fiercely that the vibrations reached Val's needles and set each shaft to shivering. A thousand penetrated nerve endings sang with pain, Val's synapses ignited and juggled fire. She writhed, and with each movement, more nerves were torched until her body shivered in the cold fire of a hundred small impalements.

And still Lettie screamed. "You're lying! You're evil and you're lying. The world's an evil place, a terrible place. Only here is where it's safe. Just here. And you and I will never leave."

That said, she crossed the room and fetched her sewing box again. A heavy picnic hamper–type box, when opened up, it revealed all that Val recalled and more—threads in a hundred colors, dull muted shades to glittering metallics, pastels diluted from the sea and sky, a dozen nuances of crimson comprising all the shades of blood—from freshly shed to tacky moist to the dull scarlet of dried gore. To go with these—a shimmering hierarchy of needles, from the thinness of a human hair to those with the length and heft of hatpins.

"This will surprise you," Lettie said, "but I'm not doing this to hurt you. I'm doing it because I want to keep you safe and wise, like I wish someone had done for me."

And she pierced a threaded needle through the skin of Val's groin. Quickly, with hands that moved so fast their speed was almost magical, a conjuror's hands, plucking miracles from the air like doves, Lettie pierced Val's labia half a dozen times in swift succession.

The pain produced was anything but magical, dazzling and sickening in equal parts. Val screamed and dug her teeth into her tongue. Lettie unscrewed the jar of honey on the breakfast tray and spooned sweetness into Val's mouth.

"You'll come to understand this later," she said, proffering honey. "You think the needles keep you bound, but it isn't really so. It isn't even the pain, although that will come to seem like pleasure, too. It's the seduction of confinement that will keep you here." She laughed, a hollow, mirthless sound that teased dread from every pore. "The day will come when I could snip every thread, remove every needle, and open the door wide, and you'd beg me not to make you go, not to turn you out into the world. You'd weep bitter tears at just the thought of being asked to leave this room."

"Try me," said Val, tasting blood and honey.

"Believe me, dear," Lettie said. "Someday you'll come to love this...especially since I'm going to teach you how to sew."

She wiped her sticky fingers on her dress and disappeared from the room. She returned a few moments later leading Majeed, who wore a chain around his neck and women's clothes. Of the two, Val guessed it was the clothing that caused the more humiliation.

"Don't worry," Lettie said. "I'm only going to hurt your lover a little bit. Enough to show you how it's done. Then it will be your turn to wield the needles."

Val shuddered with disgust. The needles in her nipples stung and tingled, their slender shafts contacting nerves that echoed in her vulva, in her womb.

"I won't do it."

"You'd be surprised," said Lettie, twirling Majeed's chain as she affixed it to a leg of the oak bed, "what people think they're incapable of doing. Even the saints are capable of the worst atrocities—it's when they recognize it that they decide to become saints. You're capable of anything. What has been done to you, believe me, you can do to others."

Lettie held a needle to the light. She squinted at the tiny eye, then sucked the end of a thread thin and white as hair plucked from a crone's head. Steel and fabric glinted in the light as Lettie carried the threaded needle back to the bed. She undid Majeed's blouse and bra, murmured something in his ear. Majeed nodded solemnly.

And then, to Val: "You'll learn to love this someday."

"No! Don't!"

Needle penetrated flesh. A drop of blood flowered on Majeed's chest. Lettie looped the needle back again and pierced the skin at the edge of one aureole.

There was a moment of pure terror when Val felt the urge to wield the needle, to bleed Majeed in every pore, a moment when she knew to her profoundest core that Lettie was right as to what she was capable of doing.

Everything.

Anything.

And it was more than she could bear.

"You fucking crazy freak! Stop it!"

Hatred galvanized her. It was her antidote for pain, and now, while fury numbed her, she bent one knee and elbow, using them for leverage, pushed up with all her strength into the needles. There was a teetering moment of agony and inheld breath when the combined strength of the needles held her down, pulling at her stretched and bleeding skin in a fresh fury of torture.

"No!"

The power of her voice infected muscle. She flung herself against the cumulative strength of the lacings in one final effort. Flesh tore as hooks and needles parted company. Blood-soaked threads broke and dangled down Val's chest and legs, while the greater part of Lettie's design, the shimmering cat's cradle, remained intact, covering her torso in a gory arabesque.

"You stupid, sick bitch!" Val swept past Majeed and knocked Lettie to the floor. Her hands flew to Lettie's neck, as they had done—in fantasy—a thousand times. The woman flailed and kicked beneath her, but there was scant conviction in her struggles. It was as if she was resigned to accept whatever fate Val deemed appropriate. Val realized her tears were dripping onto Lettie's face along with blood. Images—of midnight rides under skies so black they snuffed the stars, of haggard, frantic faces pressed against the window—"You buyin', Mama?" "You sell-in'?"—of glossy women, strutting-rolling-undulating come-ons as they did their spike-heeled sway, savage women, electrical with desperation and crackling with need, and Lettie's face, entranced and lustful as she peered out through her private looking glass to view that other world, that vast Outside, a piece of which was trapped and languishing inside her like a dead embryo, and the need was sucking Lettie dry, starving her. *You see what a terrible world it is. Just look at that. You see.*

"Oh, God," said Val, and she released Lettie's throat.

Lettie coughed up flecks of blood. "I knew it." Her voice was tiny, dry, the sound of petals being plucked from long dead flowers and crushed to powdered scent. "I knew you'd try to kill me someday. I knew you hated me."

"I did," said Val. "I wanted to kill you with my own hands. I used to plan it sitting by the window. But then you killed yourself and took away the chance."

"I hated you, too," said Lettie.

That startled Val. She'd seen herself as Lettie's victim all these years; the newspapers and magazines, the neighbors, the teams of tutting psychiatrists and clucking therapists who worked with Val after she'd been freed, had viewed it the same. As one tabloid had put it, Lettie was *The Monster Mom Who Kept Her Child in Chains*.

"I hated you for being free," said Lettie. "For seeking out the dark."

"But you're the one who showed it to me."

"To scare you, not to make you want to leave me."

"And I never have," said Val. "I've carried you around in my head like soiled clothing at the bottom of a suitcase. I've carried you in my dreams. I've hated you for being there in every place I ever went to, every bed I ever slept in. You've always been there, haunting me, spying on me, watching."

"Then forgive me," Lettie said, "and I'll go away."

"Unlock the door."

"I can't do that."

"Don't lie."

Val raised her hand up in frustration, then brought it down without delivering the blow. The accumulation of her wounding made her weak, but Lettie's sadness weakened her still more. In the shadows, Lettie's face appeared to dance with minuscule pinpricks of light that mimicked the crosshatchings of the cat's cradle.

"Forgive me," Lettie said again.

The thaw in Val, though incomplete, was tenfold more painful than the freeze, a blossoming of anguish that shivered out in razor-sharp, concentric circles from her heart. She was conscious of Majeed watching her in a trance of immobility, as silent as an inheld breath, waiting.

"I forgive you," Val said, though each word felt like it cost her a lifetime's worth of pain. "I forgive you…Mother."

Lettie might have smiled. Val never knew. The flickering sparks that strobed her face intensified. Her skin peeled back in sections, bleeding pulp and sweetness like overripe fruit. Her hands lifted up beseechingly. Val saw the tattooed palms. Her mother's face dissolved and, in its place, appeared the Berber girl's, laughing as she held up to Val the jinn-spells on her hands. That illusion lasted just an instant, though, before the child's face and body transformed again and Val was staring at the Turk's scourged flesh and ribby torso and shrunken, useless genitals. Then he, too, was gone as the room's walls folded in on themselves like the wings of origami swans. The bed, the desk, the window with its unreal view of New England fields dismantled into shreds, the shreds reduced to tatters, and these to gaudy flecks that whirled through the air like stiletto-sharp confetti.

"Filakis?" Val said, unbuckling the collar from Majeed's neck. "How does he…?"

"He's a conjuror. He fucks in any shape except his own. In his own form, he stays as chaste as any virgin. Pure. He thinks it makes him godly."

"More like Satan, I'd say."

"The City's his creation, his haven for lost souls. He's God and Satan both, here."

Val finished freeing Majeed. She plucked long needles from her chest and torso. Majeed gave her his blouse.

"Come on!"

"But the door…"

"There isn't any!"

Majeed was right. The illusion of the Sewing Room had fallen away to be replaced by the dark staircase leading up through

Filakis's prison. They lost no time in climbing it. Above ground, the City's winding alleyways were swathed in midnight dark. But if by day the inhabitants of the City had remained for the most part secluded, nightfall had changed all that.

Now bodies writhed and twisted on the cobblestones, locked in violent congress with each other and themselves, with objects, animals, and beings that, glimpsed in passing, Val could not identify as either alive or dead. If lethargy infused the sex act by day, savagery and necrophilia ruled it at night. Nor were those copulating so concentrated in their efforts that they ignored Majeed and Val. Tongues flicked out to stroke their passing flesh. Hands touched and pressed, and fingers fluttered in mute cajolement.

They avoided the on-going orgy as much as possible and plunged into the blacker corridors where, by daylight, the marketplace had offered its obscenities. Now the streets were empty of all merchandise except the human trade. In the pale illumination of a paltry moon, Val saw the abominations that the light of day had shamed into concealment. Around a heaping, stinking mound the tribe of shiteaters squatted, dining with their hands. No sooner was their vile repast consumed than their bodies evacuated the meal again, and they recommenced their feast. Forced to pass within an arm's length by the narrowness of the walls, Val and Majeed were prey to dozens of soiled fingers dangling out at them, dripping enticements as they proffered their foul treats.

Beyond that, as they approached the area of the tanneries, Majeed slipped on something in a darker patch of dark. He fell to one knee. Val stopped to help him up. Liquid ran cold and clotty on Majeed's leg. Val's hand on him came away reeking of copper. She'd barely had time to register the fact that they were skidding in a pool of blood when the moon skimmed out from under cloud cover again, revealing a huddled cluster of figures, the worst of the City's worst, the deformed and mutilated, the self-created amputees, eaters of dung and dead flesh. Val whispered something to Majeed, who'd faltered again, perhaps from shock at seeing the display in front of them.

Cannibals?

He shook his head. Less shock, thought Val, than abject fascination. Not cannibals in the truest sense, she realized, but flesheaters just the same. With razors and with small, thin-bladed knives, they sliced off tiny portions of themselves and popped these awful delicacies into their mouths, chewing with ecstatic sighs, while the men's erections hardened into steel-like batons, and sex ran down the women's legs as copious as urine. They paused in feasting only long enough to rut against each other's blood-streaked skins before returning to the next course in their macabre meal.

Val and Majeed's passing provided an unexpected distraction and the possibility for new and undiscovered flavors. The group broke apart and formed a circle around Majeed and Val. They held their razor blades and knives in fingers sliced to the bone and missing digits. It was only the clumsiness their wounding had induced that allowed Val to hurl a loose stone at the nearest one and break an opening in the circle. Majeed did the same. Another flesheater staggered back and toppled. His nearest comrade saw opportunity in this and stooped to slice off an eyelid and a speck of nose. Raw wailing rent the air.

"Come on!" Val shook Majeed. He seemed entranced but came alert when the rest of them crowded in again. Val's heart was racing, but she attributed it to fear and flight. Only as they approached the tanneries did she realize she was light-headed with lust as much as terror and that her inner muscles were clenching and unclenching in response to a steadily increasing need. The very air seemed drugged with pheromones. To breathe was to have sex. A hand reached out. Majeed.

"They're coming."

She looked behind. At first the narrow street appeared blocked by a low wall. Only when the moon performed its fan dance with the cloud again, overturning like a bowl and spilling out its light, did she recognized the "wall" to be a thing composed of flesh—night denizens of the City distracted from their coupling by the possibility of something new, fresh meat to fuck and fondle. In the mob, Val saw a few that appeared almost healthy, those who'd evidently resided in the City only a short time, but most were the derelict and drained, those far along the way to literally fucking themselves to death. The women cupped their bruised and flopping breasts, the men worked cocks made raw and scabrous from overuse, but kept erect by cock rings tight enough to bite into the flesh.

A hand slid up between Val's legs. She gasped, looked down. A hugely obese man, nude and masturbating, was crouched down in the shadow of a doorway. The sight of him—suety flesh overlapping in great grayish dollops—revolted Val, but more appalling still was her reaction to the touch. Her nerve endings keened with fresh desire. It was all she could do to kick free of her molester and dash behind Majeed into another alleyway.

Ahead she heard the approach of others closing in. She grabbed Majeed's hand and they swerved left through an ancient doorway into a dark foyer. A new smell, one Val recognized at once, assailed her nostrils.

"The tanneries," said Majeed, his hand tightening on hers.

The courtyard in which they stood was filled with immense vats dug into the ground. A heavy, suffocating odor rose up from the murky green liquid. Val felt her stomach lurch.

Outside, the stillness of the night was broken by the panting gasps of the on-coming orgiasts. In another few seconds, they'd be upon them.

"Get in," Majeed said.

"What?"

"Come on."

Holding her breath against the stench, Val followed Majeed along the slippery stepping-stones that formed narrow walkways between the vats. She heard a mucky splash, and suddenly Majeed was not beside her.

From one of the reeking vats, a voice: "Get *in*."

At the same time, from outside, other voices. The pack following them was splitting up. Val heard footfalls in the outer courtyard. Squatting down over one of the vats, she lowered herself as quietly as possible into the foul-smelling muck. Animal skins in various stages of softening swished softly around her legs as their pursuers entered the courtyard.

In the darkness, she prayed they'd be afraid to walk too near the tanning vats, that they wouldn't see her face or Majeed's lifted above the ghoulish green stew. She prayed, too, that she could stay concealed, that the mere presence of so much flesh, available and eager, would not seduce her out of hiding. In a doorway across from the vats, Val saw a couple silhouetted, locked in slow and rhythmic copulation. Barely moving, the woman hoisted up one leg around the man's thigh. He bent to take her nipple between his teeth. She fought a trembling urgency to cry out, betray herself to the mob and fall into a sea of flesh no less disgusting than the pulpy wallow in which she now was crouched.

She bit her lip against the urge. Her cunt contracted and released in pulsing, ever faster waves. The vile stench of the tannery no longer reached her brain. Instead the room was a perfumery of sex, lush and intoxicating. The woman in the doorway was writhing on her partner's penis. Her long hair swayed. Her sleek thighs clenched. Val felt the City acting on her brain like a narcotic, its mesmerizing power taking deeper hold. Its carnal wonders, even the eaters of excrement, the consumers of their own flesh, evoked less disgust now than compelling wonder and, worse, the desire to do more than look, to touch and feel, participate....

She had to get out.

The woman grinding on her lover's dick reached down to grab his buttocks. Her hands turned briefly outward. Val saw Filakis's hennaed palms. Get out now or never leave. Hoisting herself up out of the tanning vat and calling to Majeed, she sprinted past the lovers in the doorway and ran on without looking back to see what transformations might be taking place.

The streets that she and Majeed followed all led uphill, away from the City's heart. There was no more serious pursuit. By dawn, they were standing on the hillsides overlooking the earth-colored Casbah. The crenelated ramparts, towers, and courtyards lost density against the watery pastel of dawn, shimmering with ever lessening brilliance until scarcely an outline remained. To the north, another city skyline loomed, but this one curved around a wedge of dark Atlantic. Val recognized the skyline of Agadir.

Majeed caught Val's hand.

"I can't keep going."

"We'll rest then."

"That isn't what I mean."

"Then...what?"

"I think I'm making a mistake. I don't think I can...leave."

"That's crazy. If you go back, you'll die."

Majeed's gaze was rivetted on the space where vestiges of the City's walls still were faintly visible. There, silhouetted against the day, stood a lone figure. At this distance, Val couldn't see a face, but she was sure the figure was Filakis, his arms extended, pious in his mock chastity and grand in his forgiveness.

Offering that which he despised—temptations of the flesh.

"You can't, Majeed. Don't even think about it."

"I have to."

"But he tortured you."

"Yes—no. It's just a game, after all. An endless game. The torture, then the pleasure. You didn't stay there long enough to learn. You still remember how it is Outside, where the world is something besides a sex organ."

"Don't do this."

"Give me the incense burner."

"No."

"If you love me, Val, you will."

"You won't last back there. You'll die."

Majeed shrugged. "There're worse ways to die than being fucked to death."

"And me?"

"The Turk has a forgiving heart. I'm sure he'd be willing to give you another chance."

Val shook her head. She handed Majeed the incense burner and backed away. He struck a match and held it to the wick. Pale emerald leaves of fire blazed. Val shut her eyes.

When next she looked, Majeed's befouled clothes were reduced to stinking embers. The incense burner, not even charred, lay among the pitiful debris.

"Do you want to make love again?" asked Val's newest lover, a silversmith in San Miguel de Allende, Mexico. He'd come up behind her, laid his hands atop her shoulders, was rubbing his hard penis into the crack of her ass.

"I don't think so."

"Come on. I'll bet I can change your mind."

He tried to take her hand. "What's that you've got?"

She held the incense burner out to him, let him inspect it with his artist's eye, exploring its design.

"Nice carving. Where'd you get it? India?"

She shrugged and plucked the object back from him too quickly, her haste betraying a greater fondness for the artifact than for his penis, which she was already weary of examining.

"Come on now, let me suck you. Eat out your pretty pussy."

He sank to his knees. Val spread her thighs just wide enough for him to get his tongue in. She put one hand atop his head and stroked him idly. With the other, she fingered the incense burner, which smelled, she thought, though very faintly, of temptation and desire. If she held onto it, she knew the day would come when she'd no longer be able to resist its possibilities. She'd light the flame and step inside to be consumed.

Or she could pitch the object out through the open window this minute, if she wanted. Hurl it high and far and never suffer its obscene allure again. Perhaps, she thought, in time, she'd make the choice. But not yet, she thought, and stroked her lover's face. Not yet.

Unnatural Acts

"**D**id you start fucking her before or after you married me?" asked Adrienne. She stood against the mirrored wall, fists braced on satin-clad hips and confronted Bailey, who slumped on the bed, tanned and lanky in his patterned boxer shorts.

"Adrienne, does it really matter?"

"To me, it does."

"All right, if you must know. It was before. I met her at the Children's Book Illustrators' convention in Dallas about four months after you and I started seeing each other."

Six months after they'd met—Adrienne did a quick mental review. At six months, she and Bailey had been sleeping together for five and a half. They'd had sex on the living-room floor, but not yet on the butcher block table in the kitchen. At six months, they'd already spent a weekend at the Plaza, Adrienne's favorite place to stay when she was in New York, but hadn't yet visited the Broadmoor in Colorado Springs. At six months, Bailey had already started saying that he loved her, and she'd begun the game of calling him Daddy when they made love.

Bailey cleared his throat, continued, "She'd written a couple of children's books and had some questions about the illustrations. We got to talking, and it was obvious she was having some pretty major problems in her personal life. I don't see how she wrote at all, what she was going through."

But Adrienne wasn't listening anymore. The private detective she'd hired had already explained to her that Ginger Craddock's "major problem" was one Vince Craddock, husband: how Vince had served eight months in jail for aggravated assault on a pair of college kids who mouthed off at him in an Oakland bar; how since his release, Ginger had been to the hospital emergency room three times, once with a broken jaw. With hubby out of the slammer, apparently she wasn't free to go out of town to book conventions anymore. She wasn't free to do much of anything except meet with Bailey twice a week at one of the motels they frequented in Alameda.

"How often do you see her?"

"Once a week," said Bailey, after a telling pause. "No more than that."

Adrienne resisted the urge to say that didn't jibe with the detective's report, that according to the man who'd been observing Bailey ever since Adrienne became suspicious, the motel trysts took place at least twice weekly, in addition to long luncheons in out-of-the-way little restaurants, where, on at least two occasions, Ginger was seen sporting facial bruises, hands were held, and tears were shed on both sides.

She evokes both lust and pity, thought Adrienne. *The unbeatable combination.*

Adrienne moved to the window, staring out at the lights of the

Golden Gate Bridge that glittered against the night sky like a pathway made of diamonds. Her satin gown sighed around her ankles. Her black hair hung past her shoulders, framing a heart-shaped face with urchin eyes whose vulnerability was contradicted by the bitterness of her mouth, a taut gash of angry scarlet.

"Is she good?" she asked.

Bailey looked up, befuddlement rendering his chiseled features almost comical. "Good? Of course, she's good. She's been a saint, to put up with..."

"In bed, for God's sake! I don't need to ask about her moral fiber. That's already been established."

"You don't know anything about her."

"I know enough. She's sleeping with my husband. Now answer the question or would you prefer to let my imagination run wild? Is she good *in bed*?"

"You're asking is she better than you are?"

"If you choose to put it that way."

"Jesus, Adrienne, I don't know how to answer that. I suppose anyone is good in bed if you're in—"

He broke off just in time, but the import of what he'd almost said had already registered, the pain of it shocking her silent. Anyone is good in bed if *you're in love with them*.

"Do you want me to leave?" asked Bailey. "I could go to a hotel."

"Or to her?"

Was it her imagination or did his shoulders droop a little deeper, burdened with some unvoiced regret which she could only guess at?

"No, I wouldn't go to her place. You can rest assured of that."

"Because you couldn't go to her. She's married, isn't she?"

He looked up, startled, as if she'd scrutinized some tea leaves and divined his thoughts. Even now, she could still find his naiveté almost endearing, though perhaps it was not surprising in a man who made his living illustrating children's books, depicting fantasy scenes of trolls and elves and, his most successful and original creation, the monstrous Gump, protector and befriender of needy children. Bailey still didn't realize that her knowledge of his straying was anything but guesswork. He had no idea how much she knew—everything, the color of his mistress's pubic hair, her brand of sanitary napkin, the size and color of her nipples.

Brokenly now, he nodded. "Yes. She's married."

"How convenient for you. The married ones are always so much easier. They don't whine for weekends and holidays or expect flowers the day after."

His shoulder muscles corded. "Her marriage is a nightmare. The man's a brute. He's cruel. I only wish I could save her from him."

In three swift strides, Adrienne crossed the room and cracked a blow across Bailey's face hard enough to sting her hand. The skin flamed beneath his tan. She waited for him to stand. Willed him to hit her back. To fell her, make her bleed. Anything, just as long as he did *something,* made her feel something besides this excuiating, internal pain.

But his innate cowardice (that was what she called it—to Bailey, undoubtedly, not hitting back was simply being civilized) rendered him less than obliging of her need for physical response. He stared up at her, inviting another blow, and did nothing.

"I didn't do this to hurt you, Adrienne. We, neither of us, planned it. I felt sorry for her. I wanted to be her friend even though I was already involved with you. But then, of course, it turned into more than that." He bent down, began tugging faded jeans up over calves made muscular by morning runs.

"I don't blame you if you hate me. I'll sleep in the guest room tonight, if that's acceptable to you, and move out tomorrow morning."

He's leaving me.

Adrienne fought to keep the shaking from her voice, but suddenly she felt so chilled, frostbitten to her core. She thought of one of Bailey's illustrations for a book of Canadian folktales—Eskimo children, bundled against the cold with just their wide eyes showing, huddled around an insufficient fire.

And, suddenly, something inside her began a silent keening, and she was birthing pent-up pain that she'd suppressed for decades. An angry, frightened eight-year-old stood in the doorway to a house in Sacramento once again, watching as her father trudged toward the car with suitcases in hand.

I'm sorry, Adrienne. Your Mom and I don't get along. I can't stay here anymore.

A jolt of terror, pain sharp as a skinning knife against her flesh, had sent her racing out the door, hurtling down the front steps toward his car—*Wait, Daddy, please*—and near the curb, she'd flung herself forward, a desperate, stumbling leap that sent her sprawling headfirst into the edge of the open door, where he was putting in his bags, splitting her forehead open in a bloody gash.

Her calamity had bought her sympathy and time—two hours' worth—the time it took a doctor at the emergency room to calm her down and put in eighteen stitches, while she clung to her father's hand and promised to be "a good little girl" forever more, if only he would stay. But after that, her time was up. Her father took her home and returned her to a mother who felt about children as she did about zoo animals—that they belonged in cages. Then he drove away again and left her with two scars, one on her forehead that would heal, the other on her soul that stayed as raw as the day it was inflicted.

Daddy, please, don't go.

"I don't want you to leave."

Bailey looked up, eyes smudged darkly with fatigue. Extramarital adventures did not become him, she decided. At heart, he was too principled a man, so fumblingly immersed in "doing the right thing" that, inevitably, he ended up doing wrong. He looked so woebegone, so vulnerable, that Adrienne almost felt sorry for him.

"But I thought...I assumed you wouldn't want me here. Not after..."

Now was Adrienne's opportunity to make her own confession, that what she'd finally badgered him into admitting was nothing she hadn't known about for weeks. When it came to tracking infidelities, the detective that she'd hired was as eager as a hound sniffing at an unwashed groin. Her wall safe held a treasure trove of Bailey-porn: Bailey nose-deep in Ginger Craddock's mink-furred cunt, lapping up split beaver; Bailey, ever well bred and considerate, supporting his weight on his arms and thrusting with that expression of stupefied delight upon his visage that suggested religious epiphany or too many vodka tonics.

She'd trapped him and could take her choice—forgive him, take him back into her bed and heart or flay him now, cataloging his inadequacies and ineptitudes as she wiped him from her life. Except there was no choice. It was the child in Adrienne who cast the only meaningful vote, and that vote was for forgiveness. Unfaithful or not, she needed Bailey. Desired Bailey. And, God help her, loved him. She'd trapped him in his cheating not to lose him, but to bring the sordid mess to light, expose it and then, once and for all, put an end to it.

"Don't leave," she said, "I'm hurt and angry, but I never said I wanted you to go."

She untied the satin gown and let it whisper to the floor. Then she was grappling with his clothing, enclosing the ivory tube of his cock in her hand, tonguing his nipples and belly with wild hunger as they rolled back onto the bed.

"Don't go," she murmured, imploring husband and father with the same words, the sense of loss and impending loss stretching across thirty years to connect two points of unbearable abandonment. He was weak for her. She still, at least, had that. She could feel his mind and body warring, but then his cock came erect and all hesitation ended. They fucked with the kind of famished appetite that often follows intense pain and seems, in part, to justify it. In the midst of it all, while they were still joined but resting, his cock pushing inside her at a languid pace, she introduced one of her favorite games, one they'd practiced and repeated with such frequency that the lines came without embarrassment or hesitation: "Am I still Daddy's little girl?"

He hesitated. She lapped his mouth, his eyelids, caressing him with internal muscles, and asked again, and he gave in.

"Yes, you're Daddy's little girl. Do you still love your Daddy?"

She wriggled in his arms, pure animal delight. "I love my Daddy."

"And will you suck your Daddy's cock?"

"Oh, yes, I love to suck my Daddy's cock."

"And Daddy's balls? Do you love your Daddy's balls?"

"Yes, I love to kiss them, lick them, to squeeze them between my tits."

And on they went, the exchange growing ever more lewd as she described what other acts she'd do to prove her love to "Daddy" and he led her on with questions until, aroused by her responses, he commenced to thrust energetically inside her, to bite her throat and call her name.

Only when they rolled apart, each staring at their half of ceiling, did Bailey clear his throat—perhaps, she thought later, so as not to choke on the words—and say, "I can't let go of her, you know. She needs me. She loves me and…I think I love her, too."

At that moment, for the first time, she realized his affair was more than casual, that he really meant to leave her for this woman. It was like watching her father walk out the door all over again, bloodying her head in her mad dash to win him back, and still he'd left and still she was abandoned.

"No," she whispered, thinking that she would stop him even if she had to cause harm in the process.

No, she vowed and lay awake till morning.

Sometimes, in better days, Adrienne liked to joke that the matchmaker for her and Bailey's union had been her seven-year-old niece MaryAnn. Adrienne saw the child infrequently. Her brother and his wife lived in Chicago, where the couple, both attorneys, practiced law. They seldom came to San Francisco, but had flown out for a legal convention in the fall two years ago. To Adrienne, whose occupation consisted largely of a volunteer position with the Council for the Arts, had fallen the surprisingly enjoyable task of entertaining MaryAnn while her parents worked.

In answer to the question "What would you like to do today?" had come the child's mystifying but adamant response, "I want to see the Gump man."

All Adrienne could figure out was that this "Gump man," whomever or whatever he might be, came out ahead of the San Francisco Zoo and the Ghirardelli chocolate manufactory on MaryAnn's sightseeing agenda.

Finally, in desperation, she called up her sister-in-law's hotel, had her paged away from a meeting, and asked what the child was talking about.

"Oh, that's right, you don't have children, so you wouldn't know," said Staci, with that hint of righteous superiority those with children reserve for those without. Adrienne bore this condescension with great indifference. Her own childhood had been a perfectly wretched experience, and she had no wish to inflict such a thing on offspring of her own.

"She's talking about Bailey Arnes, an artist who lives on a houseboat over in Sausalito," Staci explained. "He draws the Gump, a kind of good-guy monster in a series of little kids' books. The Gump's ugly as hell. I don't know why kids love him, but MaryAnn and all her friends have Gumpamania this year. Anyway, this Arnes guy, according to the paper, he'll be in the toy department at Saks doing a signing at noon. I know MaryAnn would love to go if you don't mind waiting in line with a bunch of rugrats."

It was fine with Adrienne, who only wanted to amuse her niece and had no special preference for how she spent her Saturday.

Her enthusiasm cooled somewhat when they arrived at the store and got in line behind dozens of small children, all clutching one or more of the five Gump books and attended by adults who looked as dubious about this whole thing as did she.

The illustrator, whom Adrienne could only glimpse occasionally from her place in line, was a lean man in his mid-thirties with a runner's build. His hair was wavy and abundant, the color of wet autumn leaves. He wore a turquoise earring, a pink shirt with a flamingo pattern, and trousers that were supported by a pair of rainbow suspenders. His watch sported a T. rex on the face, but he seemed oblivious of time, spending minutes with each child and slowing the line to a crawl.

The process took far longer than Adrienne had expected. She was frazzled and impatient by the time she and MaryAnn finally approached the Gump's illustrious creator.

"And who are you?" asked Bailey Arnes, one tanned cheek dimpling when he smiled at MaryAnn.

MaryAnn, who up until this moment had been chattering away nonstop to everyone around her, suddenly turned shy. She looked away. She popped her thumb into her mouth. Adrienne gently removed it.

"Her name is MaryAnn. She's a great Gump fan."

Bailey nodded, smiling. He looked not in the least exhausted for having conversed with scores of under-eight-year-olds during the past hour. "Can I see the book you brought for me to autograph, MaryAnn?"

The child was mute. Adrienne pried the book from her hands. Bailey opened it to the first page illustration, which depicted the Gump in all his off-beat weirdness—warts, bumps, spiked cheeks, ears that looked like tufted rhino horns. He smiled at the little girl, and also—differently—at Adrienne, who experienced an unfamiliar heat deep in her pelvis. "How about if I draw you your very own personal Gump, MaryAnn?"

His voice was honeyed brandy, at once avuncular yet unabashedly seductive. His hand flew rapidly across the page, producing a small goblin that, to Adrienne, was no less hideous than its parent on the page. His hands were large and spatulate, hands Adrienne would have expected to be more skilled at tractor maintenance than art, and furred with pale blond hair. He wore several rings, none of them a wedding band. Such signs of marital status Adrienne rarely even noticed. Her last affair, with a financial consultant who ogled her not inconsiderable portfolio with the intensity that previous lovers had reserved for more intimate areas, had ended almost a year earlier. She hadn't felt the gut rush of desire in so long that the effect was almost enfeebling, like drinking too much wine too fast and suffering the consequences.

"Here you go, MaryAnn," said Bailey Arnes, handing the child her book. "You're such a smart-looking little girl. Why don't you tell me what you like about the Gump."

MaryAnn, growing bolder, considered this. "If I had the Gump to be my friend, no one bad would ever mess with me. No one could ever hurt me."

Bailey beamed. And Adrienne, in a move so uncharacteristic that even now she marveled she had ever had the courage, withdrew a business card and said, "I'm chairperson for the Council for the Arts this year, Mr. Arnes. We're always looking for interesting new speakers. I'm sure you're very busy but...I wonder if you'd call me."

He called her almost a month later, all apologies for having been on tour promoting Gump books and paraphernalia. She'd pretended to barely remember who he was, but she'd recognized his voice the minute she'd picked up the phone. That voice that made her shiver as if a hard cock had just brushed past the tip of her clitoris, that called forth more pleasure in her groin than most men she'd known were capable of producing with their entire bodies.

She had waited thirty-seven years for Bailey Arnes to come into her life. No matter what she had to do, she was not about to lose him.

On the telephone, Vince Craddock's voice was potent, too, but not in a way that Adrienne found reassuring. He sounded like a good ol' boy with an attitude, his rich baritone inflected with both impatience and a woodsy Georgia drawl, his diphthongs taking one-syllable words and smearing them into three. Twice before she'd said her name and what she wanted, Adrienne almost hung up the phone. An underlying bite in that buttery voice made her think of razor blades concealed in Halloween treats, of bonbons laced with strychnine.

"So you'd like to see an apartment, Ms....?"

"Davis," she said, giving him her maiden name. "Adrienne Davis."

He gave her an address, and they dickered briefly over a time convenient to both before settling on three P.M. For a man in the business of managing apartments, he didn't seem especially keen to show them, thought Adrienne, his tone of voice, in fact, suggesting this was more an imposition on other, more pleasant plans, than an opportunity to rent an apartment.

He asked few questions: whether she was seeking one bedroom or two, did she have pets or children (both grounds that would disqualify her as a potential tenant). Throughout, Adrienne kept wondering why she continued the charade, why not just state her purpose baldly, that she needed to speak with him about something of an urgent personal nature?

An urgent personal nature.

Somehow Adrienne was fearful he'd just laugh and hang up on her, that his was the sort of messy life rife with the urgent and the personal—to anyone but him, that he'd think she was a creditor or a jilted girlfriend shown up with babe in arms. So she upheld the fiction that she was merely looking for an apartment as they scheduled an appointment.

Before leaving the house, she stopped by Bailey's first-floor studio. It occupied a spacious room adjacent to the guest bedroom, with a sweeping view of Tiburon and Sausalito no less spectacular than that seen from the master bedroom. And nowhere were Bailey's anal-retentive tendencies more in evidence. The room was spotless and meticulously organized, more the province of an accountant than an artist. Drawing board flanked by color-coded sketch books, a computer for graphics, one whole wall stocked with bookshelves.

Bailey sat with his lean form draped across his drawing board. Next to his chair, like some kind of grotesque totem, stood a two-foot-high metal statue of the Gump. With its spiked face and warty dome, its froggish eyes and toothy maw, it looked, to Adrienne, like a gnome exposed to radiation or a vicious, retarded dwarf.

"It's because little kids feel weak and vulnerable," Bailey had once explained to her. "They like pretending to have a buddy like the Gump, even smaller than they are, but with all those spikes and claws to make him tough."

The steel Gump was a gift to Bailey from a sculptor whose three-year-old daughter had recovered from a serious illness clutching a plush, kapok-filled version of the creature.

Bailey looked up from his drawing board. "I didn't see you there."

"You were concentrating too hard. How's work going?"

"Slow. It's hard to focus when...look, about our conversation last night...I think—"

She raised a hand. "We don't have to talk about it anymore. We both said things in anger. I'm willing to forget what's happened if you'll just stop seeing her."

Bailey looked as if he'd been physically punched. "Didn't you hear anything at all I said last night?"

"Then you meant it—you won't abandon her?"

He shook his head. "I can't, Adrienne. I'm sorry."

"You expect me to share my husband?"

"No, of course not. I just think…I don't see any easy solution here. I don't want to cause you more pain, but if we stay married, I see nothing but pain for both of us."

"So you're asking for a divorce?"

"I think that would be best, yes."

"I'll think about it," she said and turned away from the door.

Fine, she'd given him a chance. His last one. If he couldn't bring himself to say good-bye to Ginger, then she'd have to help him along.

Before leaving the house, she detoured by the den, unlocked the private wall safe where she kept documents and jewelry, and selected two of her detective's most lurid photographs—both views of Bailey's back and ass, but splendid shots of Ginger, auburn tresses reaching just short of pink, poker-chip-sized nipples—and tucked them into her Gucci tote before going out the door.

The Harmony Apartment Complex on Bancroft Avenue must surely have been named by a disgruntled tenant with a sense of the absurd, thought Adrienne, as she searched for the manager's office. Despite the prohibition against children and animals, both were in obstreperous evidence, their presence requiring her to step around or over both broken toys and dog feces as she commenced her exploration. The dismal, low-set buildings were unmarked. Adrienne was forced to stop a dowdy matron with hair piled atop her head in a frowzy pineapple and ask directions to the manager's unit.

The woman produced a grimace halfway between a guffaw and a sneer.

"You want that bastard Craddock? Well, take a hint from me, honey, a lady like you don't want to live here. Cockroaches are big as lemons and you can't get them to unstopper a toilet or fix a broken pane to save your life."

When Adrienne persisted, she finally was directed to an end unit where a tiny sign, too small to be seen from the street, read MANAGER.

Vince Craddock must have been watching from the window for he opened the door while her hand was still poised to knock. His broad shoulders were packed into a pale green T-shirt. His grubby jeans bore what looked like grass and mud stains on the knees. The hand he held out to Adrienne was large and thickly veined, with grime packed beneath the nails.

"Ms. Davis?" He looked her up and down with mingled interest and suspicion. It took Adrienne a moment to realize why. She was dressed all wrong for this encounter, from her two-hundred-dollar pumps to her silk dress and pearls. No one dressed like this would be renting an apartment here.

"Come in," he said, curiosity clearly triumphing over hostility as he stared at Adrienne. His black hair was long and lank with grease. A tattoo, some complex geometry of interlocking crosses, adorned his forearm. Only his eyes were unbesmirched, tiny mosaics of topaz and emerald chips and fire. "You're right on time. That's good. I admire punctuality in a woman."

That said, he ushered her into a narrow office, oppressive with stale smoke, that contained a cluttered desk and two leather chairs. The walls were lined with file cabinets and boxes marked with the names of plumbing supply and hardware shops. He was, apparently, a jack-of-all-trades: apartment manager as well as resident fix-it man. Adrienne moved aside a stack of magazines and took a seat in the one available chair opposite the desk.

"Sorry for the mess," he said, pulling a cigarette from a pack and lighting it as he took a seat. "The maintenance man quit last week, so now I'm doin' everything from lawn care to fixin' the commodes. You smoke?"

"I quit ten years ago."

"Good girl. It's a nasty habit."

The "girl" raised her ire; she'd have walked out right then under any other circumstances. Instead she said, "Actually, I've become allergic to cigarette smoke over the years. I wonder if you'd mind not smoking."

He took a deep, long drag, blew it just above her head—the

smoke still reached her eyes, making them tear—and ground the cigarette out into an overflowing ashtray.

"So tell me, Ms. Davis," he said, leaning forward on the desk in a way that made her, almost instinctively, lean back, "what exactly did you come here for? You out slumming today? Doing some kind of exposé on slumlords for one o' them upscale papers? Cause sure as hell you ain't here to rent one of these shit-hole apartments."

She smiled thinly, working at maintaining her composure. "How perceptive of you, Mr. Craddock. I'm afraid you're right. I'm here for something else entirely."

It was an unfortunate phrasing. He reared back, black anger in those agate eyes. "You from the city—a building inspector or something?"

"No, not at all," she stammered, flustered now. "Actually I'm here because I have a problem, and I think you can help me with it."

He shifted in his seat, hand reaching automatically for the pack of cigarettes, then pulling back. "I don't like games. What's this about?"

"It's about your wife, Mr. Craddock. About Ginger."

"You know my wife?"

"Not really, but…my husband knows her all too well."

He sat back then and remained silent while she told him everything. Midway through her speech, he lit a cigarette. Adrienne made no objection.

The photos she saved for last.

"I wanted to be absolutely sure, Mr. Craddock, so I hired a private detective. The best available. This way there can be no doubt."

He examined the two photos. His facial expression stayed as impassive as one of the stone monoliths on Easter Island. When he finally spoke, he asked a question that, of all the questions possible, was the last one she would have expected.

"These private dicks, they cost a fortune, don't they? Did you pay for this with your own money? Or with your husband's?"

She wanted to say that—the Gump notwithstanding—Bailey's

monthly income as a book illustrator would barely keep them in prime rib and Dom Perignon one week, that it was her own fortune, inherited from her mother's side, that maintained their honeyed lifestyle. Of course, she said nothing of the kind. She was afraid he'd assume her to be a woman men loved only for her money. She feared that, like any natural predator, he'd sense this secret terror was her weak point and exploit it.

"I took out a loan," she lied glibly. "But that's not the issue, is it? The issue is that your wife is fucking my husband, not just as a casual fling, but a long-term affair. They're serious about each other. I want it stopped, and I think you're the one to do it."

He looked up from the photos, mouth twisted in a frightening mix of mirth and menace. "Give me your husband's name and address, and, yeah, I'll stop it. Permanently. You bet your pretty ass."

"No," she said. "My husband is my business. But you can stop your wife. I don't care how you do it. Beat her up, threaten her, just get her under control...."

He ground out his cigarette, lit another. "These photos, are these all? Or are there others? Ones that show your husband's face?"

"That's all of them."

"Bullshit!" His voice, thought Adrienne, could have caused the needle on a Richter scale to quiver. "You expect me to believe these two are all he took? If that's true, then you didn't get your money's worth. I want to see somethin' besides the crack in your husband's hairy ass. I want to see his face."

"You just do your part in this," said Adrienne, bending to pick up her purse as a prelude to leaving. "I told you I'll take care of my husband."

"By doing what? Cutting off his supply of home pussy?"

"You're out of line, Mr. Craddock. I came here to do you a favor and—"

"And I'm supposed to take care of my bitch, is that it?"

"However you want to phrase it, yes." She got to her feet, was disconcerted when he came around the desk and blocked the door. The mood was turning nasty all too quickly. *Stay calm,* she thought, *the bullies are all bluff and bluster if you just stand up to them*.

"And you just expect to dump this in my lap and then sashay out of here." He reached out and flicked a contemptuous hand across her pearls, her silk sleeve. They were close enough that she could smell his body odor, musky sweat and rancid sex, pores clogged with day-old dirt. "Back to your ritzy little life and your sorry fuck of a husband."

She stood her ground and spoke to him as she would to Bailey, "I understand that you're upset. Believe me, I was, too, when I found out. I thought it was important that you know. Now I'm leaving."

It was an error. This wasn't Bailey who blocked her way. This was someone else entirely.

"Oh, no, you don't. If I can't have the pleasure of putting my fist down your husband's throat, I can sure stick my dick up his wife's high-class cooze."

He locked the door and stepped toward her. She moved backward, but there was nowhere to go. Her rump struck the corner of the desk hard enough to make a bruise. Then he was on her. She screamed, of course, but he slapped that out of her fast, vowing to use his fist if she persisted.

"It don't matter anyhow, if anybody hears," he growled into her hair. "The tenants are all scared of me. Nobody's gonna interfere. Nobody's gonna stop me."

So it was up to her, but she saw at once that she was hopelessly overmatched—none of the tricks of self-defense she'd read about in women's magazines, none of the stratagems an overcautious Bailey had explained to her—were in the least effective. He laughed when she tried to knee him in the groin and rewarded her efforts by yanking her hair so brutally she felt hunks of it tear out. And when she attempted to drive the heel of her hand into the notch at the base of his broad throat, he let her do it, all the while maintaining the smirk upon his face, then grabbed her wrist and twisted it until she thought the bone would snap.

"Anything else you want to try?" he hissed at her. "Cause I got time. All afternoon, in fact. Which is how long I'm gonna fuck you."

He bent her back across the desk. With one hand he held her there, while with the other he swept the desktop clean. Stacks of documents that might have been leases, newspapers and correspondence, scattered to the floor. The ashtray exploded in a small Vesuvius of glass shards and flying ash.

"No, please, this serves no purpose," begged Adrienne as his hand parted her thighs, invaded the silky swatch of underpants.

And he stopped touching her.

She thought at first a miracle had happened. He'd come to his senses or, for whatever unlikely reason, her entreaties had prevailed, and he was going to let her go. He looked down at her, mouth twisted in a sneer that she found less than comforting.

"Stand up," he said, his tone of voice implying something far more ominous than her release.

She did so. He took a step back, leaned his bulk against the door, and looked her up and down in a way that, somehow, was more humiliating than his hands on her a moment earlier had been.

"Strip."

"What?" A bit of her bravura was coming back now that he'd let her up. "You must be crazy if you think that I—"

"Strip," he said, "or I will rip off your clothes and stuff them down your throat until you choke. Believe me, I don't care whether you service me dead or alive or barely alive, but you *will* service me."

She wanted to believe it was the outrageous threat of a practiced bully, but she'd felt his hands around her throat. She knew better than to put him to the test. Her hands were trembling as she began unbuttoning her dress. The tiny buttons fought her, almost as if they tried resisting, too, then came undone. The dress slithered in a pile of silk around her feet, and she was standing only in her bra and underpants, her pumps and pearls.

"Good little girl," he said, with a facsimile of sweetness that was all the more repulsive for its effect on her. She was still shaking, but her muscles relaxed a bit, as though he'd hypnotized her with a word or emptied a syringe of heroin into her unwilling vein. She could feel the seductive swish of blood in her head and groin and nipples, a warm internal bath.

"Bra next," he said.

She shut her eyes and reached for the clasp in front. Her breasts fell free.

"Please," she heard herself whisper, "no," but she was already bending, like one in a dream, to slide down her underpants.

"You can keep your shoes and pearls on," he said. "I wouldn't want you to lose your dignity."

He stepped forward, plucking at her here and there with quick, brutal touches: tweaking her nipples, tugging at her lips and ears, yanking her forward by her pubic hair into a painful embrace.

"You smell nice," he said conversationally as he shoved her around to face the desk. "You smell like an expensive whore, but I'll treat you like a cheap one."

With that he spun her around, V'd her legs, and slammed her face first into the desktop. There was a brief lull in the assault when he must have taken down his pants and booted them aside. She heard a zipper and cloth rustling, but was afraid to turn around.

Then he was penetrating her with those thick, nicotine-stained fingers. She could hear the smirk in his voice as he said, "You're wet, bitch. You're fucking dripping."

He withdrew his fingers and forced them between her lips. She could taste her own juices and his cigarettes on his flesh. His fingers were rough, like sandpaper against her gums, the inside of her cheeks. She bit down. He grunted, gulping back a howl, and brought the wounded hand down to her throat to throttle her. Points of black light capered behind her eyes. A harsh buzzing, like a mad surgeon sawing into her skull, seethed in her ears. Her pearls broke. White dots danced now among the black ones as pearls rained onto the desktop, spun and clattered to the floor.

Almost as an afterthought, she realized he had penetrated her, slamming her forward with each thrust as he used his hold on her neck for leverage. And he was talking, although, in her dazed state, she could barely make out the words. It was like listening to static-drowned voices on a distant radio.

"Is this the way your husband fucked my wife? Is that the

sound she made when he was doing her? Tell me who he is, you goddamn whore. Tell me or I'll fuck it out of you."

She made an animal sound and writhed against him. The action only served to impale her further. Then, apparently eager for some new orifice to ravish, he pulled out, spun her around, and shoved her to her knees. His penis, slick with her juices, beat an impudent tattoo against her lips. Cunt smell and cock smell, a dizzying, almost sickening bouquet of rut, assailed her.

"Open or I'll ram it through your teeth."

She had little will left to fight him, only to survive this ordeal and escape. Lips parted, she took the vile thing in where, heedless of her teeth, it battered the back of her mouth in sharp thrusts that left her gagging. And all the while he was pounding her with his penis, he kept up a verbal assault as well.

"Is this the way your husband fucked my wife's face? Is this the way she took it? Are you gonna tell him about this, whore? Or maybe just let him smell my jizz on your breath?"

The mere thought of his ejaculate shooting down her throat evoked more retching. She could not imagine drinking this man's semen. She'd as soon have swallowed excreta. Apparently his attention span was limited, however. No sooner had he threatened to come than he abandoned her mouth as well. She crouched, panting, at his feet, praying it might be over, knowing it was not.

"Stay," he said, as one might command a dog. "Don't move."

He went over to the other side of the desk, his departure opening up a clear path between Adrienne and the door. *Run, now,* her desperate mind implored, but the imperative might as well have been issued to a quadriplegic.

Escape, before he set her free, *if* he set her free, was quite simply now beyond her. But for her shoes, she was completely nude, bereft of her pearls, bruised and disheveled. Worse, though, than her physical condition was her mental one. An air of unreality had taken hold. Her adult identity—Adrienne Arnes, wife and socialite—seemed blurred and almost comically remote, like a character from a fable or fairy tale remembered from her youth in bits and snippets. The child that she had been, abused, distressed, and lonely, crouched on the floor, and passively awaited the next horror.

It came when he swung the desk chair around beside her head and rammed her mouth again. A few quick thrusts, grunting threats and curses, and he pulled out in time to spurt upon the chair seat, a process that took fully ten seconds while the pond of semen, like spillage from a carton of soured milk, grew ever larger.

On her knees, an appalled Adrienne was eye level with the spectacle. She could see the swollen vein under the shaft, the purple meat of foreskin, the head with its cyclopean eye still drooling the last drops out onto the chair seat. Suddenly her hair was seized again, her face was plunged into semen.

"Lick it up." A whisper this time, seductive, soft, as if he were inviting her to partake of some gourmet delight. "Lick it all up, like a good little girl. Or I promise, I'll make you do much worse."

She believed him. Somehow, she accomplished the foul task without puking. When she looked up, lips sheened, he was already zipping up.

"Go on. Get out of here. Go home to your cheating husband."

Numbly, she began to dress, knowing she'd discard the clothes as soon as she got home, burn them perhaps, anything to be rid of the awful tang of him. She only wished that she could do the same thing with her skin.

"One thing you ought to know," he said as she was reaching for her purse, the same gesture that had preceded his attack, in what seemed a lifetime ago. "Our little lovemaking session here didn't settle your husband's debt. He's still going to pay. Make no mistake about that. And you, I'll be fucking you again."

His expression changed then, softened somehow as though the foulness were somehow permeated with a trace of humor. He stepped forward, lifting her face up to his in the manner of a suitor seeking to memorize every detail of the beloved's features.

"You'd like that, wouldn't you? I know you would."

This last frightened her as much as anything that had gone before. "I'm calling the police," she said, wondering if this would be his cue to kill her, marveling at her own folly. But he stepped aside, performing a mocking little bow as he unlocked the door and stepped back from it.

"Call the cops, if you like. I'm sure your husband would be interested to know what you were doing here. Myself, I'd say it sounds like a revenge fuck—sauce for the goose and all that. In the meantime, I'm going home to have a talk with my wife. Do a little marriage counseling."

Adrienne stepped past him, out the door into the fading sunlight and freedom. To her departing back, he said, "You've been such a good little girl. I think I'll fuck you again real soon, honey."

Such a good little girl.

The words fell across Adrienne's departing back like lashes. She made it back to the car, locked the doors, and gave vent to anguished sobs. Her thoughts were blurred, chaotic. She felt that she was weeping, not only for the brutalizing that had just been inflicted on her, but for losses long forgotten and pain as yet ungrieved.

As though the battering had wounded not just internal walls, but punctured areas of consciousness she kept sealed off, her wracking sobs brought back a memory of her father, the only clear image of him she'd ever had except on the day he left.

She remembered being six years old, an overweight little girl already well schooled by her mother in self-loathing. Her parents hadn't parted yet. Her father was at home that Saturday, a spare, drumstick-thin man with big hands and basset-hound eyes, reading in his study. Engrossed in some kind of science fiction book. Oblivious of her.

And Adrienne was hungry.

So hungry.

For attention, love.

She remembered climbing onto her father's lap.

"Hi, honey." He had glanced down, smiling absently, continued reading.

Adrienne had shifted her position and voiced the Magic Question. "Am I Daddy's good little girl?"

His eyes were rivetted on the page. He nodded, grunted out some sort of response. Then resumed ignoring her. She began to squirm. Began to squoosh her bottom around as if she had to go. Reached down to pet that part of him she'd only glimpsed when he was coming out of the shower, closing the towel around his waist. Her father mumbled something and moved her hand away.

Adrienne put her hand right back, continued petting the lump in his lap, which felt small and soft, but clearly defined, like a chipmunk nestled underneath the cloth. Was rewarded for her persistence when something stirred, and now the chipmunk was no longer balled in sleep but stretching upward. She could feel its contours, a straight hard spine, a knobby earless head.

"Adrienne! Damn it!"

He stood up so fast that Adrienne was dumped onto the floor. She sat there, stunned, gazing up at the chipmunk in her father's pants, feeling that need to connect with him more than ever now that he was angry with her, and she reached up—

"No!"

He slapped her face. Hot, sizzling pain.

Connection.

"Don't ever do that! Ever!"

Her cheek flamed, the sensation that of sudden, acute sunburn. The hurt felt good. Her Daddy's touch. Even as the tears began, she hoped the sting would last forever. It hadn't, and she'd spent a lifetime searching for it. In Bailey's bed. In other beds.

Had found it now, in Vince Craddock's abominable embrace, a vicious parody of love. The thought caused her to curl up on the front seat of the BMW in a fetal self-embrace, knees hugged tightly to her chest, hair straggling down and pasted to her face with tears until, at last, she was calm enough to turn the key in the ignition and drive home.

Afterward, it was the scent that kept the nightmare vivid. She bathed at once upon getting home, of course, a shower first to scrub the worst of the ordeal away, then an hour-long soak in a steaming bath scented with lavender and musk. Her bruises, whether by luck or by design, were all inconspicuous. Bathed, made up, and dressed in a silk caftan, only a haggardness about the eyes, a jitteriness to her movements, betrayed the afternoon's events.

But the smell—it must have penetrated her very pores, the marrow of her bones. Not just Vince Craddock's smell, but hers as well, the odor of hothouse sex, eau de bitch in heat.

Bailey, clearly ill at ease, uncertain perhaps whether he should still be in the house at all or packing up to leave, stayed in his studio until dinnertime. His appearance then was late and apologetic, his overenjoyment of the food patently false. She could almost see him chewing guilt along with the sole almandine and new potatoes the cook Consuela had prepared.

He made no comment about Adrienne's odor nor did he question her about her whereabouts that afternoon. In all likelihood, thought Adrienne, shut up in his studio, daydreaming of his lover, he hadn't even realized she was gone. Adrienne toyed with her food, repulsed by the white sauce in which the sole filets floated, nauseated by the bodily reek the Poison she was wearing failed to mask.

"I'm going out," said Bailey, rising from his chair.

The fear in her eyes must have halted him.

"Just for a bit," he said quickly. "I need to walk off this meal." Then, perhaps groping for some banality that would soften his exit, he added, "I'll stop by the kitchen and tell Consuela how much I liked the sole."

He picked up his unused spoon, dipped it into the sauce remaining on the fish platter, and took a slow, contemplative taste of the creamy liquid. "What is this anyway, beurre blanc?"

Adrienne just looked at him, eyes hollow.

But her stomach voiced its own opinion of his spooning the pale goop into his mouth. She bent double and suddenly vomited copiously onto the Oriental carpet.

The next morning, Bailey was already up and about when Adrienne dragged herself downstairs. She paused for a moment before the tank of tropical fish in the hallway, gazing at the serenely finning angel and butterfly fish and the small, turquoise tangs, and tried to reclaim some sense of calm. She was haggard and puffy-eyed, her body sore inside and out, her brief bouts of sleep having been the cue for every demon from her subconscious to caper forth, a veritable Mardi Gras of nightmares.

The worst of the nocturnal horrors had come just before dawn. She'd awakened with the need to empty her bladder (the piss felt like fire on her abraded genitals) and, returning to bed, had fallen prey to a nightmare so immediate and vivid that her unconscious mind had no time to register, however dimly, that it was, indeed, a dream.

She had found herself crouched down in a murky corridor, gazing into a room illuminated at the far end. The view was dizzily kaleidoscopic—everything fragmented and shifting as though the room and its occupants were in a state of slow but steady revolution. Yet even so, she recognized the furnishings immediately. It was the bridal suite at the Fairmont Hotel, a spacious room with Tiffany lamps and an ornate, antique armoire, walls enlivened with fey and precious Fragonard nudes, and a vast bed with a white canopy like the spread wings of a silken swan. She and Bailey had spent a weekend there shortly after they were married. Perhaps Bailey had found the rococo extravagance of the suite inspiring; she scarcely recalled a time when his lovemaking had been more passionate.

To Adrienne's frustration, the room's two occupants appeared less well defined than its furnishings. They seemed to coalesce from solid shadow, performing a languid mating of mouths and genitals like shadow puppets whose lewd display was projected against the pale rose wallpaper. Wraith limbs elongated and intertwined in their ghostly coupling.

Straining to get a better view, she tried to enter the room herself, but was restrained by a wall as thin and clear as cellophane, yet impenetrable as steel. As Adrienne watched, the woman reversed her position to sit astride the man, breasts lolling downward to cover his face. The man's tongue thrust into her cleavage. He reached back and grasped the woman's buttocks, parted her and penetrated her with his fingers.

The mosaic of colors broke apart and shifted. The shadows swirled again. Now Adrienne could see only a blurred tangle of limbs and torsos interlocking, breaking contact and reconnecting like pieces in some complex kinetic sculpture. Like living versions of the erotic carvings on an Indian temple, the faceless couple went through a complex, sometimes perverse, repertoire, coiling finally into a human donut to perform *soix-ante-neuf* in a frenzy of lapping, gobbling, suckling, slobbering. They bucked and slithered like two shiny reptiles busily attempting to ingest each other.

Another shifting and re-making of the shadows: now the woman knelt, head down, her rump raised for the taking. Her mate impaled her with strokes worthy of a swordmaster, until, after Adrienne thought surely he must climax, he pulled out and exercised his other option, buggering her lustily. His final act (and the one which woke Adrienne up in icy shivers) was to use his cock to penetrate portions of his mate's anatomy that had no natural orifices. His bladelike member pierced and rooted here and there, his withdrawal followed by a spew of blood and raw, fleshy tidbits that resembled sushi. And still he wasn't sated but roved about her thrashing form, redesigning her anatomy in the most grotesque ways.

Appalled, transfixed, Adrienne viewed it all. But what was it she was seeing? She tried to glimpse the woman's face, but her writhing—now considerably lessened since her mate had penetrated both cheeks and was busy face-fucking her from a most unconventional direction—kept her head turned away from Adrienne. The man, however, was clearly a psychopath as powerfully inclined to murder as to mating.

Despite the horror of the scene, Adrienne found herself fascinated. She couldn't look away. Indeed, she wanted to get closer, to smell the blood and dip her fist into the woman's wounds, to probe the punctures with hands and tongue and sample of the fleshfeast. Instead, she woke up with her fingers thrusting deep inside herself, still smelling of Vince Craddock.

After a night of such vicarious debauchery, she was even less prepared to deal with the gloom written clearly on Bailey's face when she finally appeared for breakfast. He was slumped defeatedly before a plate of toast and melon wedges as pristine as when Consuela had set it on the table, staring into space with the dull distress of a man standing on a ledge, exhorted by the crowd below to leap and get it over with.

She spoke to him, but was awarded no reciprocal good morning. Adrienne realized he was grub white, almost malarial in his pallor and that sweat stood out in greasy beads around his forehead.

"Bailey, are you all right?"

She noticed with some distaste that the stains from last night's stomach upset were still clearly visible on the costly carpet. Her eyes were drawn there, anything so as not to have to look at Bailey's face.

"I said are you—"

"No. I'm not all right." He shook his head, pushed himself up shakily from the table. "Something awful's happened."

She was afraid he was going to faint and moved around the table to support him. In doing so, she saw the newspaper where he had let it fall. Some instinct—apprehension, hope?—allowed her to leave Bailey to his own devices and peruse the page. Continued strife in the Mideast, an outbreak of Hepatitis B traced to a seafood restaurant at Fishermans' Wharf, in Berkeley a murder/suicide...

Oh dear God, no.

(*Oh, yes!*)

She scanned the article: Around 8 P.M. the night before, a neighbor had heard screams and a gunshot and summoned the police to the home of apartment manager Vince Craddock, forty-four, and his wife Ginger Craddock, thirty-six. The door was locked, but police forced their way inside. They found the body of Ginger Craddock, dead of blunt trauma to the head and multiple stab wounds, next to that of her husband Vince, who'd shot himself in the head with a Colt .45 revolver. An investigation was continuing but neighbors reported Craddock to be a man of violent disposition. Police had been called to the house several times that year to quell domestic arguments.

So there it was, thought Adrienne, her nightmare of the phallus/knife. The dream was real and had made the headlines. Dimly, she was aware of two things: that she had been holding her breath the whole time she read the article, the result being that now she felt quite lightheaded and that Bailey, standing rigid before the dining room's bay window with its view of lushly verdant Tiburon, was sobbing quietly.

"I can't believe this. It's so horrible."

"Things like this never make any sense," said Adrienne. "The husband must have been a madman."

"From what she told me…the things he used to do to her, they were unbelievable. He used sex as a form of torture. But still, I never thought that…."

"I'm sorry, really," said Adrienne. "I know how much this hurts you."

Bailey's voice shook. He seemed to be on the verge of hyperventilating. "I talked to her just yesterday. She sounded so…so happy."

"Yesterday? You mean you called her after I went out yesterday afternoon?"

"I thought I should let her know that…that I had told you I was having an affair. I needed to talk to her, and I knew the bastard she was married to was at work. She told me lately he'd been more abusive than ever. She was making plans to leave him. She said she felt like she had a brand-new life ahead of her, and all she had to do was walk out the door. And now…"

"And I suppose you were that 'brand-new life' she wanted?"

It came out with more venom than she intended.

"She was going to a battered women's shelter, someplace he wouldn't be able to find her. After that…"

"You were going to leave me for her, weren't you?"

"I don't know, Adrienne. My mind's stopped now. I don't know what I was going to do. Only that I'd promised I wouldn't leave her. And now she's dead, and I feel like it's all my fault."

"I can't believe this." She knew this was the wrong time for what she was about to say, that a tragedy had taken place—one in which she had played a pivotal role—but the words seemed to leap from her lips, lemminglike into the void of silence. "You act like she's some kind of innocent, like she was ambushed in an alley by a lunatic. She was *married* to this man, she lived with him. She had to know how dangerous he was. Yet she chose to fuck around behind his back. So what happened was the logical outcome of two choices that she made: her decision to stay with an abusive husband and her decision to commit adultery. I don't see why such stupidity merits so much sympathy."

Bailey looked up, devastation etched upon his face, his eyes brimming with tears.

"It almost sounds like you think she got what she deserved."

"Of course not. It's just that…I'm sure she's not the only one who's suffered at the hands of a sadist. She's not the first woman who was ever abused."

"I can't believe I'm hearing this. Can't you understand, she's *dead*, and her death was horrible? Can you even imagine what those last few minutes must have been like for her? Who knows what he may have done to her before he…Oh Jesus, don't you understand? I loved her, no matter how wrong that might seem to you."

Adrienne tasted acid. "Of course you were in love with her. How could you resist? She was the needy little waif. You were the would-be knight. I see where I went wrong now, my love. I was never sufficiently pathetic to get your rescue fantasies all stirred up. I never managed to fuck up my life sufficiently to win your pity." Her voice rose. Consuela, coming out of the kitchen with a pot of coffee, froze like a rabbit caught in headlight beams before retreating to the kitchen. And still, Adrienne could not muster the will to silence the rush of sarcasm. "I know what! I could give all my money away to charity. I could make myself destitute, so you'd have to buy me little thrift-store frocks and then maybe I could find a lover who'd beat me up occasionally. You could weep over my black eyes and my poverty and play the knight in shining armor come to rescue the fair maid. It makes you feel important, manly, doesn't it? Too bad your armor is as tarnished as your honor."

She dared him with her eyes. As usual, it was he who broke eye contact first, who backed off from her challenge.

"I'm sorry, I have to get out of here. Ginger's dead and you're screaming nonsense. I can't be with you now."

And he was gone, pulling on his overcoat and trudging out into a morning opaque with fog. Adrienne watched him from the window, the fog shifting around him like ocean currents, making it almost appear that he was walking underwater. She remembered how she had watched her father leave her thirty years before. Desperately she wanted to run after him, to cry and beg forgiveness for whatever she'd done wrong, but such a ploy hadn't moved her own father not to leave her and would scarcely be effective on a husband grief-stricken over the loss of his lover.

Besides, though she was loathe to admit it, even to herself, there was the matter of…her odor. She was afraid Bailey would smell her, if she got too close. How could he not? Despite a half hour in the bath, she was still perfumed, not with the scent of lilac bath oil beads, but with cum and sweat and bodily secretions, the odor of a female animal in estrus. She could smell sex, wafting up from her vagina and swirling around her body like the fog.

The murder/suicide of Vince and Ginger Craddock garnered a few more paragraphs in the next day's *Chronicle* and a spot on the six o'clock news in which a local women's advocate reiterated the need for women mated to violent men to seek shelter at a halfway house and neighbors, predictably, described Vince Craddock as a surly, distant man, a loner. Within days, however, other, more newsworthy crimes made headlines and Adrienne no longer had to fear seeing pictures of the murderer and his victim-wife every time she opened up a paper or turned on the news.

Still, she could think of little else. At times, she found herself gazing out the window or staring into the fish tank and murmuring, "It wasn't my fault, it wasn't," like a mantra that would become true if oft enough repeated. Vince Craddock was a dangerous man, she knew from personal enough experience. He already beat his wife; he'd have killed her sooner or later, and maybe Bailey, too, if he'd ever caught them together.

It wasn't my fault, she thought, but even as the enormity of what she'd set in motion left her guilt-stricken, there was another part, less easily acknowledged, that frankly celebrated her rival's death, that would have shed her clothes and capered through the house singing "Ding dong, the witch is dead," had propriety and her own self-consciousness permitted such a thing.

Meanwhile, Bailey wandered the house like a brain-damaged blind man in stumbling search of some unseen exit. Small tasks obsessed him. He fed the fish so often Adrienne worried that he'd kill them, mulled aimlessly about the garden, and experimented with various combinations of elbow grease and cleaners to remove the vomit stains from the dining-room carpet. Only the absence of scars at his receding hairline argued against the conclusion that he'd undergone a recent lobotomy. To Adrienne, he was polite and formal, like a boarder behind in rent who feels his presence imposes on the others in the household.

With Ginger dead, Adrienne decided she could afford to be magnanimous. Her outburst of the day before had served no purpose, had only succeeded in driving a greater wedge between Bailey and herself.

"We don't have to make love," she said, leading him, at last, to bed. "Just hold me."

It was a lie. Her appetite for him was as keen-edged as a week's worth of hunger. Since the morning when she'd awakened from her dream to discover Ginger and her husband dead, her appetite for sex had grown with every hour. Several times a day she filled the tub with bubbles and took long soaks, stroking herself to luxurious orgasm, caressing breasts and belly, slick with suds. No amount of self-pleasuring, however, was adequate replacement for what she really craved.

Her obnoxious odor seemed to have diminished, either that or she had found a combination of perfumes successful at masking it. Once in bed with Bailey, she snuggled against him, taking comfort in the heft and brawn of him, the sweet solidity. He draped an arm around her, she kissed her way along his chest, then slid beneath the covers. She found him unaroused and went to work to change that. He recoiled and pushed her head away.

"Please. Just let me sleep."

"What about me?"

"You said you only wanted me to hold you."

Regretfully, she abandoned her efforts on behalf of his erection. *Be chaste as you can stand,* she thought. *But see how long you can be faithful to a dead woman when a live one's right beside you.*

Bailey sighed and flung an arm across her. "I'm sorry, I just can't make love," he muttered and soon commenced snoring.

"I love you," whispered Adrienne to his closed eyes.

It was going to be all right, though, she decided. Even with that small gesture of his arm across her chest, he was coming back to her. She'd done the right thing by telling Vince Craddock what was going on. He was a monster who deserved to die, who'd have killed Ginger sooner or later anyway and maybe Bailey, too. Thinking this, she fell asleep.

And into dreams where she was no longer a voyeur, but the main event. She was inside the bridal suite this time, wrists secured to one of the bedposts. Other ropes, more for adornment than function, evidently, bound her chest, circling each breast so that the flesh was deeply grooved, the nipples jutting up and out at a painful angle.

From behind her: *I can smell you, whore. That's how I'll always find you.*

Vince Craddock pressed his face to hers. He murmured soft endearments interspersed with the filthiest obscenities, then forced a knee between her legs. She fought him, gripped her thighs together, until he looped a portion of the rope around her neck and tightened it until bed and walls and flesh all turned to water and her legs, no longer under her command, floated open like languid dolphins.

Then he was ripping past her sphincter muscles, clutching her bound breasts for leverage as he thrust into her, his grunts competing with her screams to make a monstrous harmony. The bridal suite, in the meantime, had lost none of its kaleidoscopic splendor. Each object in the room, each portion of anatomy resembled fluid mosaics with the capacity to disassemble and reform in an eyeblink. Thus even as the sodomy continued, a new defilement was already in the forming. She lay upon the bed now, the agony in her rectum no less severe for the surrealness of her surroundings.

Vince straddled her chest. He held his penis at the base and whipped it back and forth across her face. *You're pretty, but you stink of sex. I think I'll give you some of ol' Vince's special per-*

fume. Piss shot into her face, her lips. It gleamed in her black hair like opals. Then he was striking her, heavy metronomic blows that forced her head from side to side, until she screamed, not from the pain but the perverse humiliation—that with every blow, uncontrollably, she orgasmed.

After that, he became her tender lover for a while, all sweet concern and kisses, until the kaleidoscope took another twist and she was on her knees, using her tongue to penetrate a portion of his anatomy that she would scarcely have consented willingly to touch without the use of rubber gloves. He returned the favor with a variety of objects, heated metal, icy steel, all the while making promises of more and worse to come. Promises which he took leisurely pleasure in fulfilling. Depravity upon depravity, all interspersed with the tenderest endearments, the softest of caresses before the mood changed and once again she was the victim of the vilest of unnatural acts, some that drew tears and blood, others designed merely to subdue, humiliate.

Waking from these dreams, she was exhausted and unutterably drained. And yet, no matter how hard she fought sleep each night, it inevitably came, plunging her into new and more atrocious torments.

But if Adrienne slept too deeply and too long, Bailey—to all appearances—slept little at all. Gray satchels pouched beneath his eyes. His skin was slack and sallow, like a man afester with inner contamination. On the few occasions when Adrienne awakened in the night, she'd find him sitting up, eyes open, staring into darkness.

Once, still half-mesmerized by the power of her dreams, she longed to unburden herself, to confess: *I caused it. I killed your lover as much as if I'd used the knife myself. But I'm a victim, too. Vince Craddock raped me, and he keeps on doing it—night after night while you lie there pining for your lost love.*

To admit to such a thing, of course, would win her little sympathy, would forfeit any hope of reclaiming her husband's affection and so instead, she tried another tack, to seduce him out of mourning with tiny tastes of what she, however much against her will, was learning to appreciate.

Lying next to him, she whispered, "Did you and Ginger do things in bed we haven't? Is that what made you want her? That she was willing to do things you thought would have repelled me?"

She was surprised how easily she could say Ginger's name, but then, she thought, the dead don't exist, not really. They pose no threat. What need was there for jealousy?

Now she prodded Bailey gently, "Was that it? Was she a wilder partner?"

"I don't know what you mean by wild. She was passionate, intense. But when all two people's time together is stolen, it's...sweeter, I suppose."

"But were there things you did together that we don't?"

"Meaning what?"

"Games, fantasies. What some, I suppose, might call perversions?"

"Really, Adrienne, I'm uncomfortable with this."

She slid a hand up under his pajama tops and caressed her way along the ladder of his belly. Seduction honeyed her voice. "There must be things you'd like to do to me. Things that maybe Ginger's husband did to her and that she told you about. Things you wanted to do but were afraid—"

"Jesus, Adrienne." He pushed her hand away. "There was nothing especially exotic that we did in bed, if that's what you're getting at. And it wasn't just all sex, you understand. Sex was the least of it. Why does everything come down to sex with you? Why can't it ever be love?"

Because love is a lie, she thought, *even the love between parents and their children. It's all sentimental pap, romantic fiction. But sex is real and makes a passable substitute for love. One starves anyway, but at least sex stills the hunger.*

But to say this was beyond her.

"Please, Adrienne, let's just go to sleep."

She, too, felt exhausted, but at the thought of what lurid dreams awaited her, her hands and hips developed an agenda of their own. She spooned herself against the wall of Bailey's back, pressed her breasts to his shoulder blades, described serpentines against his buttocks with her groin.

For all the response she got, he might as well have been a corpse.

Then suddenly she understood. Of course, he was rejecting her. She stank, reeked like an unwashed whore. While he, having spent part of the afternoon at work upon the carpet, smelled faintly of Lysol and a variety of other stain removers. Rising from the bed, she went into the bathroom and douched and scrubbed and douched again, perfumed herself anew. When she returned and pelted Bailey's neck and shoulders with kisses, he sighed and turned to face her.

"I can't sleep. I've been lying here thinking. I know I'm pushing you away, and I know that isn't fair. It's just that I'm so upset, half-crazed with guilt. All I can think of is how it must have been for Ginger at the end, and how I might have stopped it, if I'd insisted that she leave him but...I know there was nothing I could have done. And I know all this has been terrible for you, too."

"It has been terrible. I have bad dreams. So bad I can't describe them."

"I know," he said. "Last night I heard you sobbing in your sleep."

He put his face into her hair, whiffed at her neck. "You wear too much perfume these days. The whole house smells of Poison."

"I only wanted to smell nice for you," she said. "So that you'd want me. I know you're mourning her, but you can still desire me."

Bailey embraced her then, in a companionable way. After a while, embracing turned into rubbing, suckling, which ignited a mutual need that led to ardent lovemaking. On her final orgasm, Adrienne lapsed into darkness for a while. When she opened her eyes, she lay sprawled out on that other bed, ensnared in webs of shifting light and mesmerizing color.

In Vince's arms.

I knew you'd come to me. I smelled you. He slurped his tongue across her cheek, over one eye, then down across the other, webbing her lashes with saliva. The sensation was that a plump snail had dragged itself across her face, leaving a trail of slime.

"Are you your Daddy's little girl? Do you belong to Daddy?"

She screamed. He laughed and pinned her down, affixing apparatus to her body like a gleeful and sadistic child: cold clamps for her nipples, manacles for her wrists, steel rings for her labia that pinched and pulled and jangled. With that, the kaleidoscope began to turn, their bodies disassembling and reforming into positions ever more exquisitely painful and exotic. Ropes came to life in Vincent's fists. They undulated like charmed snakes as he bound her in the most adroit and elegant and torturous of ways, all designed to offer maximum discomfort while providing him with access to every crevice, every orifice.

Appalled, she found her body capable of new and horrifying possibilities. With little prodding, her jaw unhinged to accommodate his fist. He penetrated mouth and throat, then groped beyond. She felt harsh fingers scrape her heart and wind around her ventricles. Blunt knuckles bruised her lungs.

Then he withdrew, plucking soft, internal pieces between his fingers as he did so, and made it up to her for his mistreatment. He covered her with kisses and sweet nibbles, all peppered with a myriad of pet names and obscenities.

Until the colors rotated and reformed into another act, this time a series of new defilements that left her body outraged and her mind numbed, and she was bleeding from both her natural orifices and half a dozen others that were of Vince's own creation and with each drop of blood, she shivered out a tiny, exquisite orgasm and lost a fragment of her soul.

But Vince, it seemed, was wounded, too, as grievously as she. When she dared open her eyes again, she saw that half his skull was blown away, exposing a pulpy wonderland of gray and yellow matter. He tipped his head, dislodging bits of skull. Brain matter sloshed, dripped down.

It's your fault, you know. You caused it all to happen.

Her mouth, a shattered thing, gaped open like a baby bird's. The awful treats dripped down, tasting of salt and copper, and she was...

...screaming and...

...Vince was shaking her, chunks of him coming lose and pelting down on her, a patter of vile sludge.

"No, please, Vince, no, I'm sorry! I never should have talked to you. I never should have told you."

He let her go as though she were on fire. A moment earlier, she'd felt his fingers on her shoulders. Now they were gone.

And the kaleidoscopic colors changed again, expanding outward with dizzying complexity. Colors, sounds, and textures replicated themselves in an infinity of variations and from her vulva rose the sweetest, most beguiling of fragrances. She bent forward to clutch her ankles and leaned down to lick the sweetness from her inner petals.

I can smell your pussy, whispered Vince, somewhere close by. *If I can smell you, I can find you.*

She came awake abruptly. Her perfume was a memory. Her body reeked again, the sick whore smell of body fluids rank with disease.

Downstairs, something thudded to the floor.

"Bailey? Did you hear…?"

But her groping hand touched only sheets and mattress. He was gone. Somehow, the idea that he had left her bed at 2 A.M. was more profoundly terrifying than her original belief, that the house had been invaded by a prowler.

She got up, belting her robe around her, and traced the noises—small ones now, the minor stirrings of someone shuffling about in an otherwise silent house—to Bailey's first-floor studio.

To her amazement, he was fully dressed, wearing jeans, loafers, and a patterned workshirt, and he was busy sorting through his sketchpads and canvases, boxing things away. His immaculate studio now looked like a playroom in which a child has thrown a tantrum: sketchbooks and drawing pads flung helter-skelter on the floor, a box of charcoals reduced to powder, as though they had been stomped. The statue of the Gump had been moved over by the door. Maybe the Gump was standing guard, thought Adrienne, for such as she, but if so, her husband needed a keener-sighted sentry. The short, spike-headed Gump stood next to Adrienne in mute complicity, brute-looking arms hanging at pudgy sides, porcine nose and froggy eyes protruding from its studded face.

His back to her, Bailey removed a photo from his desk and studied it. Even at a distance, Adrienne could see enough to know that the close-up of a woman's face, a tanned oval framed in orange hair, was that of Ginger Craddock. Somehow this sight, coming upon her husband in the throes of pining over the dead woman's photograph, was more wrenching to Adrienne than if she'd surprised the living lovers cavorting in her bed. At least she might have taken action then, be it tears or physical assault. Perhaps, too, she had misjudged the power of the dead. Perhaps real flesh, she thought, held no enticement equal to the allure of memory.

"What are you doing?"

Startled, Bailey spun around, the look on his face suggesting a man caught masturbating into his wife's underwear. He fumbled the photograph back into his desk as Adrienne came into the room.

"Bailey, it's the middle of the night."

"I know. I couldn't sleep."

"I heard you thumping about down here."

"I dropped some boxes."

"Come back to bed. I need you. I had another nightmare, the worst one yet."

She wrapped her arms around his waist, determined to prove to him that, however sweet might be the memories in a photograph, she could promise something else. She was changed now and could offer him debaucheries and defilements beside which love would appear to be the paltriest of pleasures. He pulled away. She feared it was her stench appalling him, but so great was her desire that she persisted.

"Bailey, please, I want you."

He shoved her backward, hard enough that she would have fallen had her back not thudded up against the wall.

"I know about the nightmare. You were crying, talking in your sleep."

She forced her lips into a moue of innocence. "It was a dream. I don't know what I said."

"I do. You woke me up. You said 'I shouldn't have come to see you' and you called out the name Vince."

"I don't see what…"

"Adrienne, my God, you talked to Ginger's husband, didn't you? You must have told him everything. That's why he killed her." He came closer, lifted both hands as though to seize her throat, then changed direction at the last instant and slammed his fists into the wall. "Christ Almighty, how *could* you?"

"I don't know what you're talking about."

"Fine. All right. I'm getting out of here tonight. I won't spend another minute under the same roof with you. And I'll file for a divorce tomorrow."

"You can't mean that."

She clutched at him. He shook her off with a look of such loathing that she felt real fear.

"Don't ever, ever touch me again, Adrienne, or I don't know what I'll do. As far as I'm concerned, you killed Ginger. It isn't safe for me to be around you now."

"You want me to admit it then? All right, I will. I knew about your lousy affair long before you admitted it. And, yes, I went to Craddock. I even showed him pictures my detective took. I'm glad he killed her, Bailey. I only wish I could have done it myself. The way he did it—with a knife!"

Bailey stared at her as though she were metamorphosing before his eyes into some kind of beast.

"My God," he murmured, awestruck, "you are a monster."

He turned his back to her, suitcase in hand, and started up the hall. Adrienne watched his departing back, superimposed upon her father's back, both turned away, both leaving her forever.

Dear God, stop him, don't let him go, cried the child in Adrienne. *Don't let him leave me. Not again.*

It was no deity, however, but the wretched Gump who came to Adrienne's rescue. Children were right about the Gump, it seemed. He truly was a friend to those in desperate need. Suddenly, as miraculously as any fantasy in one of Bailey's drawings, the Gump launched himself into the air and struck with a resounding clomp at his creator's departing head. Blood spewed. Bailey slumped against the wall, groaning words that came out mush, perhaps a plea to his creation to let him live.

If so, the Gump was, indeed, an ingrate and deaf to all entreaties. Metal spikes and nodules tore at flesh, tiny hooked hands plucked lips and eyes. The Gump proved a relentless warrior. When he was through, Bailey's gouged and flattened face resembled a grotesque caricature of the Gump's lumpen and distorted visage.

Adrienne knelt beside him in her bloodstained bathrobe. "Bailey?"

She'd been holding the Gump by its toadish feet. Now she let him fall. Two cheekspikes snapped off and skidded along the polished floor like metal thorns. The hallway reeked of blood and worse—in death, Bailey's body was leaking all the grosser scents that flesh is heir to.

Yet Adrienne, covering her face, smelled something that surmounted even these. Her own odor, wafting up from her groin, stinking like a plague pit. She thought of putrescent fish ripening on a sunny dock, of whores infected with venereal diseases, reeking of cum and discharge and diseased menstrual blood.

The sheer force of the odor left her poleaxed. She crouched beside her husband's corpse, until a voice, not far away, murmured, *I can still smell you.*

The words were as vivid as the gore on Bailey's bone-white scalp. She looked up and saw, behind the vertical column of the fish tank, a roiling, seething, of the shadows. The fish, wild with agitation, had begun to swim in frantic figure eights. Some leaped high out of the water but were foiled in their attempt at flight by the tank's top. Other, smaller fish, retreated to the crevices of rocks and sunken castles and hid there, as though the shadow of a shark had passed across their pink gravel floor.

Adrienne realized suddenly that the fish weren't really fish at all, but pieces in an elaborate, floating jigsaw, each one bearing part of Vince's features. Black dots that had been spots on a passing angelfish were suddenly recognizable as eyes. The striping on a sergeant major she saw for what it really was—his grinning and misshapen mouth. Vince stuck out a sluglike tongue and swished it against the glass.

If I can smell you, I can find you.

Clean.

She had to clean herself. Excise the odor from her flesh at any cost.

Bailey had already done much of the work for her. With his obsessive cleaning of the vomit stain, he'd assembled a formidable array of cleaning products. Preparing them, she thought, was not unlike a mixologist concocting some new and gloriously potent cocktail. The difference merely lay in which lips drank the drink.

Vince watched her fill the rubber bag. He didn't speak or move, but Adrienne was not deceived. She saw his outline in the foliage pattern—jungle vines intertwining with broad-leafed palms—on the green and yellow shower curtain in the upstairs bath. Adrienne lay back inside the tub and let the pinkish venom drain down the tube and through the nozzle thrust high inside her.

Clean. I've got to get clean. It was like being fucked with jagged glass. Her flesh began to burn, internal tissue searing.

She howled and...

...took the tube into her mouth and...

...drank until all protest was scorched from her throat and her howls were quieted to desperate gasps.

For Bailey.

For her Daddy.

But the one who finally came to meet her, moving toward her through a tunnel that throbbed and pulsated like a bloodred birth canal, offered little in the way of consolation. He made only vile promises, of debaucheries to learn and pain to come and kisses that would hurt forever.

Whispering *I knew you'd come. I knew you'd come to Daddy,* Vince came to claim his bride.

PAT CALIFIA
SENSUOUS MAGIC
A Guide for Adventurous Lovers

Pat Califia provides this honest peek behind the mask of dominant/submissive sexuality—an adventurous world of pleasure and personal exploration too often obscured by ignorance and fear. With wit and insight, Califia demystifies "the scene" for the novice, explaining the terminology and techniques behind many misunderstood behaviors. Califia proves invaluable in dispelling the negative, oppressive mythology built up around S/M. The adventurous (or just plain curious) lover won't want to miss this ultimate "how to" volume.

131-4/$12.95

SKIN TWO
THE BEST OF SKIN TWO
Edited by Tim Woodward

For over a decade, Skin Two has served as the bible of the sexual sophisticate.. Editor Tim Woodward has consistently brought together the most diverse collection of artists, writers, and visionaries to contribute to this singular conception of sexuality at the cutting edge of culture.

130-6/$12.95

MARCO VASSI
THE SALINE SOLUTION

During the Sexual Revolution, Marco Vassi established himself as an intrepid explorer of an uncharted sexual landscape—his erotic adventures and the philosophy he built upon them made him a sensation. During this time he also distinguished himself as a novelist, producing *The Saline Solution* to great acclaim. With the story of one couple's brief affair and the events that lead them to desperately reassess their lives, Vassi examines the dangers of intimacy in an age of extraordinary freedom

.   180-2/$12.95

THE EROTIC COMEDIES

A collection of stories from America's premier erotic philosopher. Marco Vassi was a dedicated iconoclast, and The Erotic Comedies marked a high point in his literary career. Scathing and humorous, these stories reflect Vassi's belief in the power and primacy of Eros in life, as well as his commitment to the elimination of personal repression through carnal indulgence

.   136-5/$12.95

A DRIVING PASSION

"Let me leave you with A Driving Passion. It is, in effect, an overview of all his other books, and my hope is that it will lead readers to explore the bold contribution of Marco Vassi."

—Norman Mailer

Marco Vassi was one of this century's great sexual explorers. His writing questioned received notions of sexuality and pushed the boundaries of eroticism further than even the Sexual Revolutionaries would have imagined. But while he was known and respected as a novelist, Vassi was also an effective and compelling speaker. A Driving Passion collects the insight Vassi brought to his lectures, and distills the philosophy that made him an underground sensation.

134-9/$12.95

THE STONED APOCALYPSE

"...Marco Vassi is our champion sexual energist."   —VLS

During his lifetime, Marco Vassi was hailed as America's premier erotic writer and most worthy successor to Henry Miller. His work was praised by writers as diverse as Gore Vidal and Norman Mailer, and his reputation was worldwide. The Stoned Apocalypse is Vassi's autobiography, financed by his other groundbreaking erotic writing. Chronicling a cross-country trip through America's erotic byways, it offers a rare glimpse of a generation's sexual imagination.

132-2/$12.95

Richard Kasak Books are available from fine booksellers or
Phone: 1 800 458-9640   Fax: 212 986-7355

MASQUERADE BOOKS
801 Second Avenue, New York, NY 10017

Charge your order via MasterCard or Visa, or send a check or money order plus $1.00 for the first book, 50¢ for each additional book. Please allow 4–6 weeks for delivery. NY residents add 8 1/4 % sales tax.